HERTZ GETS FUSED

SUZANNE PURVIS

OWL'S NEST PUBLISHERS

OWL'S NEST
PUBLISHERS

Est. 2021
Owl's Nest Publishers
P. O. Box 63
Cross Plains, WI 53528
owlsnestpublishers.com

Cover Design & Images: Ash Schlax
Chapter Images: Ash Schlax
Title Font: Ash Schlax
Text Font: Century Gothic

ISBN: 978-1-957362-09-0 (paperback)

Hertz Gets Fused / by Suzanne Purvis
After accidentally torching his room, twelve-year-old tech-obsessed Hertz Zindler is sentenced to a summer in nowhere Arizona with no technology, no friends, and no way off the local sheriff's suspect list for a recent string of arsons.

Printed in the United States of America

HERTZ GETS FUSED

SUZANNE PURVIS

PRAISE FOR HERTZ GETS FUSED

"What do you get when you cross a tech-obsessed boy with a slow-motion town like Show Low, Arizona? You get HERTZ GETS FUSED: a delightful, heartfelt story filled with warmth, humor, chaos, and more than a few disasters. Hertz is a high-energy, kind-hearted kid, with a wide imagination and a knack for finding himself in the hot seat. When Hertz accidentally causes a fire at home, a summer in Show Low, Arizona is the result—along with weeks of being tech-free. At first, Hertz can't imagine how he'll cope...but with the help of some new friends and the wise, sage, laid-back "Pops" at his side (and his beloved dog, Avis), Hertz discovers what life is like unplugged—and it's not so bad at all." —Kelly Bingham, author of *Shark Girl*

"Filled with humor, heart, high energy, new friendships, fast action and adventure, *Hertz Gets Fused* is sure to appeal to kids looking for an emotionally engaging and ultimately upbeat read." —Cordelia Jensen, author of *Skyscraping, Every Shiny Thing,* and *The Way the Light Bends*

Dedicated to
Skylar, Jessica, and Jim

Trouble

Smoke. Flames. Sirens.

Godzilla-sized trouble.
Cleaning-toilets-til-I'm-a-hundred trouble.
No-allowance-in-this-millennium trouble.

From half-way down our puny cul-de-sac,
sparks spit and crack.
Smoke huffs and puffs.
Orange flames flick.
In and out of a window.
My window.

The caveman fight-or-flight thing
floods my blood.
But I don't move.
I'm grounded.
Likely grounded for life.

Delay the Launch of the Truth Starship

Mom grips my arm like Iron Man.
Mom's blind. Sight-impaired,
she only smells and hears
the blaze
that erupted
while
we were out for
our evening walk
with her guide dog, Avis.

At least
she can't watch
our small ranch house
turn to ash.

"Hertz, what's burning?"
Mom's panic tone is 30 percent.

Whoooooooosh. Bleeep. Bleeeep.
South Phoenix Firetruck No. 4
arrives on the scene.

Avis lifts his nose,
sniffs.
He knows.

"Hertz? Was that a fire truck?"
Mom's panic hits sixty.

My guts churn.
I might puke.

I suck breaths,
wheeze
like my friend Ben
having an asthma attack.
Could I have got asthma
in the last two minutes?

Mom urges me
down the street.
Toward our house.
Toward my doom.
Her head tilts,
concentrating on sounds:

> *Firefighters trudging*
> *across our gravel yard.*
> *The wrench attaching*
> *hose to hydrant.*

I walk super slow.
Funeral march slow.

"Is the Dula's shed on fire?"
Mom prods me to walk faster.

"Nope. Not the shed."

"Is it the Corkum's garage?"
"Nope. Not the garage."

On our tiny cul-de-sac,
only three houses sit
at the bubble end,
the Dula's, Corkum's, and ours.

I delay my launch
of the truth starship.
Drag my feet.
Hope like heck in
firefighters vs flames,
firefighters win.
Fast.

Nosy, Vulture Neighbor

Ancient Mrs. Corkum swoops.
She's nosy,
hobbit-size,
and slinks up on you,
in rhinestone-studded,
fluorescent pink
sneakers.
"Can't believe how much smoke could come from
one window," she squawks.

"What window?"
Mom's 80 percent panic,
her voice like a cat's mating pitch.

"Hertz's window,"
the vulture squeals.

"Hertz's room is on fire?"
Mom's 100 percent hysterical.

Vulture Corkum
holds up her phone.
"I bet this'll
go viral," she caws.

I wish my head would drop off
zombie-style,
roll under the firetruck, and
explode.

The Fire's Not Epic

No explosions.
No roof caving in.
No walls tumbling down.

Avis and I watch a tsunami-sized stream of water
gush
from the firefighters' fat hose
through my broken window.
My stomach drops to my knees.

Water equals death
to my three gaming systems,
two computers,
one flatscreen,
and
my phoooooone.
My shoulders sag.
My chest caves.
My leg bones dissolve like wet cotton candy.
I better sit.
Then I remember my perfect,
worn-in gaming chair,
my stomach launches dinner—
Mom's three-alarm chili.

A Phoenix TV news crew
arrives,
cameras focused
on flames,
on Avis,
on me.

Sixty-second news bite
and they're gone.

Sweaty Fireman

Smoke drifts.
Hoses coil.
One firetruck chugs away.

Not much evidence of disaster.
One window gone.
Two rows of charred brick.
No smell of smoke.
Only the stench
of my mother-of-all mess-ups.

Mom walks over,
hanging on the arm of a sweaty fireman—
basketball-tall, in rubber pants.
The taps of her cane
like firing-squad bullets.

She looks almost normal,
except
her white shirt has black smudges.
Probably from Sweaty Fireman's arm.
Her hair's mussed.
Probably because she twists it when she's upset.
And her jaw's pulled tighter than the button
on my too small jeans.
Probably to hold back a
Hertz-look-what-you've-done-now scream.

Her cane touches my sneaker.
"The fire's out.
Thanks to Mrs. Corkum calling

9-1-1 so quickly."
For once, I'm glad for
bossy, yappy, snoopy Vulture Corkum.
But then Mom says,
"This is Lieutenant Woods.
He'd like to speak to you.
After that, I'll meet you inside."

My heart crashes
into the black hole of my chest.
I'm heading
into seventh grade,
but this feels
like first grade
in Principal Wooten's office
after Sherman, my pet mouse,
was found in Miss Ansley's book bag.
No. This is worse. Much worse.
The Sherman incident times-a-million.

Sweaty Fireman looks like a dad.
I've never had a father-son lecture,
but I sense I'm in for something close.
And possibly jail time.

I battle zombies, vampires, aliens—
I can handle Sweaty Fireman.
I engage my energy shield.

Sweaty Fireman steps close.
Too close.
"All the damage
was contained to your room
because it's behind

the garage's block wall.
You were lucky."
He's all facts,
but he shoots a
you-could-have-killed-someone glare.

My energy shield dissolves.
Did he say I'm lucky?

Then he holds up
not-one-of-my-best decisions
pinched between his hotdog-sized fingers.
A penny.
"You understand putting this penny
behind the fuse to your room
was foolish and dangerous?"
says Fireman Einstein.

Sure, I get it *now*.
How
our old house
equals
older wiring
equals
not enough power
to my room
equals
me solution-searching
equals
finding an
old penny trick
to boost the current
equals
DISASTER.

"Yes, sir, I understand."
Avis nudges my hand,
in support of my truth-telling.
And I'm hoping that's the
end
of Sweaty Fireman's lecture.

Nope.

His face scrunches
into an intense scowl.
"All those electronic devices plugged
into one extension cord was
what kept blowing the fuse and
ultimately started the fire."

I drop my head in shame.
Avis drops his nose
in solidarity.

Sweaty Fireman sighs.
"Your mom says you're a good kid.
And it must not be easy…"
He glances at Avis sitting tall
by my side,
still wearing his service harness.

I don't want pity.
I want a firetruck-sized crater
to open so I can dive in.
Head first.

Sweaty Fireman tosses the penny.
"Keep this as a reminder."

Because my best sports are played
on a screen,
the room-wrecker penny
bounces
off my wrist,
rolls,
lands
on the sewer grate.
I pick it up,
pretty sure
I don't
want a reminder
of my monster mistake.

Night Folds Over the Cul-de-Sac

Sweaty Fireman heads to his truck.

I blow out a breath
big enough to take out
fifty birthday candles.

Now,
how
to apologize
to Mom.

I'll take my time
going inside.
Let her and the house cool off.
About three years should be good.

"Come on, Avis. Busy. Busy."
Which is guide-dog code
for go pee, or poo.
I take off his harness.

Being a black Labrador Retriever,
Avis blends
into the dark night
folding over the cul-de-sac.

Sweaty Fireman's truck
grinds into gear.

Vulture Corkum's
still got her phone out,

still videoing my
still smoking room.
Another glance
at my broken window,
my broken world.

Screeeeech! Brakes.

Yeeeeeeeeeelp! Avis.

Emergency Vet Clinic

Please. Please. Please.
Let Avis be all right.
Murmuring prayers bubble
inside my hollow chest.

The waiting room reeks
like a herd of wet wooly mammoths
splashed through a river of bleach.

Let Avis be okay.
Just let him be okay.
Please let the dog gods hear.

I press, press, press
the disaster penny
into my palm.
Hurts.
But I'd ram a dull pencil
through my hand
if Avis would just—
please be okay.

A woman in blue scrubs
opens the door,
calls our last name.
"Zindler?"

Mom grips my arm,
I move forward on Jell-O legs,
speak our help-mom-see directions.
"Door. Three yards."

Blue Scrubs strides ahead.

"Four yards. Then right," I say.

Blue Scrubs stops.

Forget butterflies
flittering
in my stomach,
the entire Coyote's hockey team
is in there
whacking
slap shots.

Blue scrubs opens a door.

Avis.
On a tall steel table.
Not moving.
Eyes closed.
His paw
wrapped in white gauze,
a tube snaking down,
a clear bag of something
on a grim metal stand.

The grey-haired lady
with a stethoscope says,
"Avis will be happy to see you."

At the sound of his name,
his eyes open,
he lifts his head,
and yawns.

"Awwwwwwwww, Avis,
you're alive!"
The Coyotes
in my stomach
put down their sticks,
skate to the bench.

Thank you, thank you, dog gods.

Summer-Destroyer Cannon Fires

Mom shoots words-of-death.
No screens.
No gaming.
No computer.
No phone.
My brain numbs.
Then come words about
a great-uncle
I've never met.
My summer prison warden?

Mom smacks the toaster's button.
Sliced bread disappears.
More words.

She's going to Texas.
Training with a new dog.
I'm going to Show Low, Arizona.
To stay with my never-before-seen great-uncle.
For a month.

Avis snores
under the table.
I rub a bare foot across
his warm paw.

Even though I know the answer—
know
I don't deserve it—
I try.
"What about my idea?

Going to gaming camp with Ben?
He's my best friend.
He needs me there."

POP!
Toaster erupts.
Avis bolts,
hits his head,
yelps.

"It's okay, buddy.
It's only the toaster."
I dangle my fingers.
Avis licks the peanut butter.

The vet was right.
Weird, loud noises sometimes
freak out Avis.
The vet called it
post-traumatic stress disorder.
Avis has PTSD.
Because of me.

Alien Relative

"Hertzog Zindler."

I freeze like
I've been slashed
by Jack Frost's ice sword
in my *Arctic Balattica* video game.

Someone's using my full name
in a not-Mom voice
and I'm caught with
my head in a duffle bag
and only wearing underwear.

"This is Pops. He's your great-uncle,"
Mom says.

I dive
behind the couch.
"*Mom.*
A little privacy, please."

In the doorway
of the living room—
my makeshift bedroom—
Mom.
Linked arm-in-arm with a guy
who is almost bald.
The guy is grinning so wide
the lower half of his face
is just
teeth.

White-grey tufts stick
out
over his ears,
under his nose,
above his eyes.
Might be hair
or frayed wire
or small rodents.
The rodent over his right eye twitches.
Might be a wink.

"We'll be
in the kitchen," Mom says.

I dress and drag
my feet
to my doom.

"There's my great-nephew."
Pops squashes me
in a scored-the-winning-touchdown man-hug.
Pounds my back
like he's trying to dislodge
a stuck gumball.
"Good to meet you, Hertzog."

"Um. It's Hertz."
My voice is muffled in his shirt.
"I hurt you? Sorry."
Pops steps back.

"No. My name.
It's Hertz.
H-E-R-T-Z."

The rodent tufts over Pops's eyes spike.
"Gotcha. My parents
christened me
Eugene October Hertzog.
Now there's a name
asking to be changed.
Didn't take long—
second grade.
Became Pops
after an unfortunate incident
with a popsicle."
The rodent winks.
"You ready to co-pilot Anastasia?"

We're in the middle of Arizona.
I'm assuming Anastasia's not a boat.
I study the guy for clues.
He's dressed
like he raided
Walmart's July 4th sale.
Dark blue cargo shorts.
White shirt printed
with scenes of Mount Rushmore.
Red socks with white stars
pulled up to his knees.
He's supposed to be my great-uncle.
But he could be an alien
who went overboard on his
American-guy disguise.
Anastasia's probably not a boat,
but I'm not ruling out
spaceship.

Anastasia's Not a Spaceship

"She's the greatest American car ever made."
Pops pats the hood.

"Wowza Watusie. Never seen anything
quite so astonishing."
It's nosy Mrs. Corkum in her sneaky, pink sneakers.
"She's Old Glory on wheels."

I inspect Anastasia.
Just a car,
the size of four VWs
painted to match Pops.
Dark blue hood covered
in fist-sized white stars.
Bumper-to-bumper wavy, foot-high,
red and white stripes.
On the trunk, an eagle—
wings spread wide.

Pops clamps a hand on my shoulder.
"You like her?"

"She sure is rocking
the patriotic vibe.
Why not call the car Uncle Sam?"

"Her name's a long story,
something I can share
on our four-hour drive
to Show Low."

Yippee.

On The Road

After a hundred mom-hugs
and a trillion
be good and behaves,
Pops steers Anastasia
out of our neighborhood.
Me in front.
Avis snoring in back.
We merge into Phoenix traffic
crammed with cars and trucks and—
"Watch out." I grab the armrest
like it could have braking power.

Pops taps my arm. "Calm down.
I'm plenty experienced.
Over fifty years driving."

My heart bangs back into rhythm.
"Sorry. I don't spend much time in cars.
Unless you count *Cartoon Car Thieves*
which I'm awesome at."

"Makes sense.
Your mom doesn't drive.
I'm happy to teach you."

"Teach me what?"

"How to drive."

"I'm only twelve."

"I learned when I was ten."
Pops zooms through
a never-gonna-make-the-yellow,
definitely-turns-red traffic light.
"Anastasia's got some power
because she's a..."
he points to a metallic wreath
sticking up from the gigantic hood.

I know it's not a Ford.
Even though Pops and Henry Ford
might've been school buddies.

"CAD-I-LLAC,"
he says each syllable slow.
"Developed and built right here
in the U-S of A."

"With superb fuel economy too."
I mimic a hybrid car commercial.

Pops frowns. "Not so much.
She was built in 1972
when gas was
forty cents a gallon."

Hours and hours and hours and
nothing but cacti
on gravel hills.
Pops whistling along to an
old folks' radio station
playing deep-voiced singers—
Tony, Frank, and Dean.
Only interrupted by commercials for

laxatives, commemorative gold coins, and funeral insurance.

My fingers itch and twitch,
missing my phone.
I'd give my left foot
for a phone
or even a Tamagotchi
or an ancient Game Boy.
Anything by Nintendo.
Anything with a
screeeeeeeeeeeeen.

On the Side of the Road

WOOF. WOOF.

My eyes pop open.
Must've dozed.

We're stopped.
On the shoulder.
Old-man muttering.
Maybe swearing.
Through the windshield—S M O K E!

"Avis! Fire!"
I leap out,
throw open the back door.

Avis scrambles across
red leather,
bounds onto grass.

I drop in the ditch.

Avis squats beside me
and pees.

Pops hauls up the humungous hood.
More S M O K E.

"Pops, run.
Anastasia's on FIRE."
My panic—99 percent,
chimp-screech.

I run to the back of the car.
Must find water, hose, fire extinguisher.

I dive into the cave-like trunk.
Crash head-first into a red toolbox.
Search
and toss
a blanket
(*that* would've made for a softer landing),
black cables with big clips on the end,
an empty gas can,
a shovel,
a blue tarp.

"Water,
water,
we need water."
Finally,
I find
fire-quenching
Sprite.
Two-liters.

I heave myself out of the trunk,
scrape my leg on a pipe
sticking out of Anastasia's under butt,
but don't yelp.

Untwist the cap with only my un-virtual muscle.
"Hang on, Pops,
I'm coming!"
I trip
over a black sssssssssssssnake.

"Ahhhhhhhhhh. A rattler!"

I look again.
Not a rattlesnake—cables.
The bulging-black rattle
and the raging-red head
mutate back into
cable clips
lying
still
on the ground.

I stumble to the smoking hood.
Blood drips into my shoe.
"Stand back."

I splash Sprite
on the smoke-spewing geyser.

Anastasia
steams,
hisses,
spits,
and belches
a burnt lemon stink.

Pops laughs so hard,
I swear he farts.

Where's the NASCAR Pit Crew?

Pops corrals his guffaws.
"Anastasia's not on fire,
just overheated.
Steam, not smoke.
But I like your quick thinking."

I look down at my likely
gashed-to-the-bone leg.
No blood.
Sticky Sprite.

I check the road.
Both ways.
"There's nothing here."
No Starbucks.
No McDonalds.
No gas station.
We're stranded.
"Did you call
roadside assistance?"

"No need.
Besides,
I forgot the phone."

"No phoooooooooooooone?"
My chimp-shriek hits 1000 percent.

"We'll be fine."
Pops heads to the open trunk.

"We're not fine."
I rub sweaty palms on my shorts.
"Your best-American-car-ever-made is busted,
and we don't have a phone."
My voice cracks.
I sound like a girl.
I don't care.
The tall pine trees on
either side of the road
transform into
a dark, deep, scary, forbidden forest.
"Are there bears? Or Aragog in those trees?"

"Plenty of wildlife
on the Mogollon Rim."
Pops holds up
the red, now-dented-from-my-head toolbox.
"Don't worry, this is all we need."

I search the road
for help—
a NASCAR pit crew or
Hagrid.

Show Low Sheriff

BLEEEEEEEEEEEEEP. BLEEP.
Avis jerks, jolts,
barks and barks and barks.

"Calm down, big guy."
I use my PTSD-soothing voice.
"Just a cop
and he'll at least have a phone."

Pops mumbles.
Sounds like,
"Nosey Show Low Sheriff."

Out of the patrol car slides an
I-really-love-donuts cop with
Aviator sunglasses on a blumpy nose.
Hand on a holstered gun.
"That dog should be leashed."

I want to say Avis is a highly trained
guide dog who just happens to have
PTSD but instead I say,
"Yes, sir."

"Unleashed dogs can find themselves
at the Show Low Animal Shelter."
His tone sure isn't
do-you-need-help-stuck-here-on-the-side-of-the-road friendly,
more like get-the-heck-out-of-town mean.

"We'll be on our way shortly, Sheriff.

Car overheated.
My great-nephew and I plan to change out the thermostat."
Pops looks at me.

I check over my shoulder.
Still no NASCAR pit crew.

"Good luck to ya."
The sheriff squats back into his car.
"Can't get my kid interested in
anything but his phone."

My thumbs twitch,
and teary,
missing-my-phone feelings
hit—hard.

Singing Wrench

Pops digs in the toolbox,
pulls out shiny silver.
"Man's best friend.
The ratchet wrench."

Avis nudges Pops, reminding him
who's man's best friend.

Pops spins the handle,
Whirrrrrrr.
"The song of freedom."

Betting on another America-the-great lecture,
I step back. But
Pops hands me the tool.
Which I drop.
"Ow. Ow. Ow."
I wag my likely broken foot.

Pops picks up the demon tool.

I give him an
I-ain't-touching-that-thing glare.

He waves at Anastasia's innards.
"See those bolts?
They aren't coming off by themselves."
He slaps the devil-wrench into my palm.
"And remember,
righty tighty. Lefty loosey."

"I don't know anything about
bolts, or
loose gooses and
tight underwear.
But if we had a phone
I could search car repair."

"Forget the phone."
Pops guides my hand,
clutching the ratchet thingy,
into an oily metal jungle of car parts.
"You put the cylinder end
over the bolt."
He jerks my hand
in half-moons.
The wrench sings.
Cli-i-i-i-i-ck, whirrrr,
cli-i-i-ick, whirrrr,
cli-i-i-ick.
"Turning the bolt left,
you loosen it," Pops says.
"Lefty loosey.
Turning right, tightens.
Righty tighty."

"No Mother Goose sayings
that rhyme with clockwise?" I say.

"See you got the family's wise-guy gene."
Pops rodent-winks. "Could be from me."

A million instructions.
A million knuckle bounces
over cheese grater engine parts,

and Pops announces,
"There's the thermostat."
Like he discovered intergalactic colonists
hiding in Anastasia's guts.

More tools.
More knuckle scrapes,
but
I
uproot the thermostat.
I
install a new one.
Righty tight.
And Anastasia rumbles back to life.
"Okay, Pops, let's slide."

"Gotcha." Pops shifts into gear.
"Gonna slide
like a bacon-greased guy
on a water ride."

I laugh.
This patriotic,
could-be-an-alien relative
is definitely weird.
But funny.

Now, I just need to find
his phone.

Bye, Bye Burger King

So long, McDonalds.
Adiós, Taco Bell.
My stomach gurgles, grumbles, gripes.
Pops zooms past every deep-fryer drive-thru
known to kid-kind.
Then a Fish Shack.
"Pops, I'm so hungry
I'd brave pufferfish poison."

"No need for that level of courage."
Pops accelerates into a blind curve,
swerves demolition derby style.

My whining stomach leaps and
says hello to my tonsils.

Stones ping-pong off
the gravel parking lot,
Anastasia's under-belly,
and we slam to a stop.

Pops jumps out,
grabs his backside,
slaps twice,
ducks back in.
"Almost forgot my wallet.
Let's go. I'm buying.
Pancake Sundaes."

My taste buds were psyched
for charred meat,

but a pancake sundae?
Sounds like a carnival for my mouth.
I get out.
Avis whines,
gives me his sad eyes.
"Pops, maybe you could order for me
and bring it out.
I can't leave Avis."

"Course you can't leave him.
Avis is a guide dog and a hero.
Pete has a soft spot for heroes."

I could remind Pops Avis is a retired guide dog but,
"Avis a hero?"

"Sure. Was all over
the world-wide web."

My chest tightens like I'm in a T-rex death-grip.
With no connection to TV or internet,
I'd forgotten
the news crew, Vulture Corkum's cell phone streaming.
The whole state (country, universe?!)
witnessed
my ten second plunge
down the media rabbit hole?
"Pops, I'm not sure—"

"I am. You're gonna love Pete
and his pancakes."
Pops is at the door.

T-rex crushes my ribs,

but my stomach moans.
Avis bumps my butt.

Only two cars in the parking lot—
I can hide in a corner
behind a big menu.
Plus, there's bound to be a TV.
A screen.
I haven't seen a screen
in a hundred years.

No Health Inspector

No TV.
No big menus.
One long counter.
A dozen black stools.
An open kitchen.
A chalkboard the size of Anastasia's hood
hangs, front and center,
scrawled with the name
of every known pancake in the galaxy.
I scout out the farthest stools.

Pops latches onto my shoulder,
steers me straight ahead,
toward two guys
flipping pancakes.
"Pete. This is my great-nephew, Hertz."

I expect the shorter, rounder,
gray-haired guy to be Pete.
Nope. He's the other one—
super tall, young, blonde dreadlocks.
"Pops. How are ya?" His gaze drops to Avis.
"Are you bringing a dog in here?"

"He's a guide dog,"
Pops says as if Pete should know.
"My niece in Phoenix is blind."

"I don't see a niece," Pete says.

I grip Avis's collar tight.

No guide dog harness.
He's just a regular dog.
I get
ready to turn,
ready to run.

Pete laughs.
Deep, low yuk-yuks.
"Just kidding. Hey, Francis."
He's talking to the short cook.
"Health inspector due in here?"

"Nah. It's Saturday.
And he'd be too busy citing your hair
to notice a dog."
Francis flips two pancakes at once.

Pete yuk-yuks again.
"You heard Francis. Sit."

I slide onto a stool.
"Avis, sit."

Avis slides to a sit,
then sprawls flat on cool tile.

"No way," Pete says.
"Your dog is Avis?
And you're Hertz?"

Oh, no, no, no, no, no.
Pete's recognized me,
likely thanks to Vulture Corkum.
My throat shuts to tick-size.

"I can't believe it. Hertz and Avis.
Like the car rental companies?"
Pete's words melt
into a slurry of yuk-yuks.

Praise be to Thor
or the Goddess of Pancakes.
My airways open and
I can breathe.
I've heard it before so I say,
"Never ask a TV-addicted
eight-year-old to name a dog."

Pete wipes his eyes. "I get it.
Had three Chihuahuas growing up.
Huey, Louie, and Dewey."

I don't get it,
but I smile a big we're-dog-buddies grin.

Best in the State

The restaurant's not busy.
Two old guys scarf pancakes.
An older lady and a girl
my age share
a colossal plate of golden flapjacks.
Two high-school-aged dudes sip sodas,
scroll through their phones.

OMG. Phones.
My bones, muscles, and blood thrum.
I swear my cells sense the Wi-Fi.

But I can almost forget about
my lost, fried phone
because the place smells like
the inside of a chocolate chip cookie.
My starving stomach squeals.

Whack.
Pops slaps my spine,
points at a framed certificate.
"What'd I tell you.
Best Pancake Sundae in the state."

Pete pours coffee.
"You look like a smart kid.
You probably figured out
this is the only place in the state
you can get a pancake sundae."

"We'll take two," Pops says.

I add six sugar packets to the coffee Pete poured,
a whole pitcher of cream,
pick up my cup—
hand shakes.
Coffee tidal wave heads overboard.
Slurp.

Hot! Hot! Hot!

The evil brew scorches every mouth molecule.
Tongue swells,
teeth ache,
throat blisters,
but I hold in zombie shrieks because
the girl my age
walks over.

"Aren't you handsome."
She's talking to Avis.

Avis gives up all male dignity,
rolls on his back, legs in the air.

"Aw. You want your belly scratched."
The girl rakes
ladybug-painted fingernails
through Avis's tummy fur.

His tail swipes the floor faster than
Francis whisking pancake batter.

"You're such a good boy."
The girl fusses over him.

My scalded mouth can't make spit,
can't make words.

The girl finishes Avis's spa massage.
"See you later, handsome."
She's definitely talking to Avis.

Pancake Palooza

"Sundaes up."
Pete places a plate
stacked with pancakes.
And strawberries.
And blueberries.
And bananas.
And bacon.
And chopped peanuts scattered
like they were fired from a nut cannon.
And a fist-sized scoop of whipped cream.
And a pink cherry.
And running down the mountain of yum—
chocolate sauce,
caramel sauce,
and high-fructose corn syrup
masquerading as maple syrup.

Pops smacks his lips.
"Worth the drive from Phoenix?"

My head nods,
mouth drools,
fork digs in.
Taste buds are hit.
Wow, wow, wow.
Forget about fires,
life-destroying pennies,
and spending a month in the Land of Snooze.
I gobble pancake-y goodness
until my stomach presses so hard
I'm afraid the button of my jeans might shoot off

and take out Pete's eye.

A pink cherry is the only thing
left on Pops's plate.
He takes a half-eaten pancake
from my plate and
offers it to Avis who swallows without chewing.
"He's not supposed to have human food."
I parrot the guide dog instructor.

Pops holds out another pancake.
"He's retired. Like me.
Deserves a treat after all his hard work."

Avis gulps down the so-not-official dog treat.
What the heck.
I give him Pops's abandoned cherry
and go to the restroom.
I return to find my plate clean and
Avis snoring louder
than a slumbering dragon.

Pete picks up empty plates.
"Thanks for stopping in.
Hope to see you two again soon."

"No doubt about it."
Pops jingles his keys.

Avis stands and stretches,
bows, and pukes.
A half-digested mess of
pancakes
and a pink cherry

spreads
at my feet.

Dog Vomit Slide

I hold my breath,
afraid I might hurl.

"Dis-gust-ing,"
says one of the teenage dudes.

Pete comes around the counter.
"Jordan, isn't it about time you left?
Unless you and Matt want to mop—"

"We're going.
Can't stick around with this stink."
Jordan and Matt walk my way,
wave a phone in my face.
"Hey. I know you.
You're that fire-kid
who almost killed his dog."

A jolt of get-me-the-heck-outta-here
shoots to my feet—
they take off,
cartoon-style
and skid in
dog puke.
Butt hits floor.
Regurgitated pancake goo spews.
The undigested cherry sails
and lands.
On. My. Crotch.

Jordan and Matt howl.

I pray.
For a twister
to transport me
anywhere but here.
Even Flying-monkey Land
would be better than Show Low, Arizona.

Landing at Ponderosa Pines

Pops drives a mile to
Ponderosa Pines Leisure Park
into a gravel lot,
and parks beside a
mini-Anastasia—
a red, white, and blue golf cart.

"We take Sheila from here," Pops says.
"No cars in the park.
You can drive."

"Told you I don't drive."
But I slide onto the blue vinyl seat and
grip the wheel.
I'm a decent video arcade driver
and *Mario Cart* winner—
I can
probably
handle Sheila.

Avis lies on the floor
of the passenger side.
Pops sits, stretches his legs over Avis.
"What you waiting for? Turn the key."

I do,
and with leprechaun lightness,
press the gas.
Nothing.
I try with hobbit-foot force and
we rocket

straight toward
a space-shuttle-sized tree.

"Brake. Brake. Braaaaaaaake!"
Pops hollers.

I slam the other pedal.
Stop a gerbil's breath from tree bark.

Avis woofs.

Pops slaps his heart.

I check if I peed my shorts.
"You'd better drive."

"Nonsense. Give it a chance," Pops says.
"Give it all a chance.
Driving, Show Low, me."
Pops holds out
his knobby, knuckled hand,
"Let's shake on it."

We pump up and down.

I'm stuck far from video game camp,
without my computer or phone,
but Pops is okay.

Plus, he's bound to have
a flat screen TV.
And I'll find—and likely have to charge—his phone.

Then...all will be right in the world.

Driving Lesson

"Put Sheila in reverse."
Pops adjusts his
Proud-to-be-an-American cap
lower over his eyes.
Probably so he won't have to
watch.

I flip the switch to R,
step on the gas,
bump over a tree root,
brake just before
I smash into Anastasia.

Pops wipes his neck with a cloth
that likely dates back to
the Pilgrims.
"Careful of my girls.
The gas pedal's a little touchy."

I shed my shoe.
Barefoot,
I master Sheila's temperamental pedal.

Coasting along white gravel paths,
I can almost pretend
I'm in virtual reality.
Me—Luke Skywalker,
if Luke were in a distant nebula,
where he drove a golf cart
instead of an X-wing fighter.

I spy a bunch of thirty-foot long shiny tin cans
hiding in the trees.
"What is this? A dump site for used missiles?"

"Nope, Airstream trailers.
Another great American innovation."
Pops gears up his history-lesson vibe.
"Did you know in 1929 Wally Byam
purchased a Model T Ford chassis
and built the first towable trailer?"

I turn—
a bit fast,
a bit wide—
knocking over a rabbit crossing sign
clearly hung too low, and
not very secure.
I swerve back onto the path.

"Hey. You hit my sign."
A grey-haired guy in overalls
shakes his fist.

Pops waves.
"We'll straighten the sign later, Earl.
Teaching my great-nephew how to drive."

Driving for real
is not as easy as keeping Mario or Luigi
on their racetrack.

We pass more tin can trailers
without crashing into trees
or knocking over signs.

My toes have the touch.

"You're doing great," Pops says.
"Back to Wally Byam.
Did you know he published
How to Build a Trailer for One Hundred Dollars?"

I didn't know.
I don't want to know.
But I'd love a hundred bucks.
I could reconnect with the world.
A used laptop maybe,
or an old game system,
or a two-year-old phone.

"Just look at the aerodynamic effectiveness," Pops says.
"Wally figured out the Airstream profile
has over 20 percent more towing efficiency
than standard box trailers."
Pops is spouting trivia like a gameshow contestant.
"And did you know 70 percent
of all the Airstream trailers ever built
are still on the road?
Now that's environmentally friendly."

He's gushing
too much math
and history
and science.
My summer-vacation-brain is
going to explode.

Red-hatted Gnome

"Treeeeeeeeeeee!" Pops grabs the dash.

I stomp the brake.
A little late.
Sheila smacks into a mailbox.
"It's still standing," I say.

"Hurry up. Reverse.
That's the Park President's mailbox,"
Pops says.

I reverse,
hit the gas and—
Whuuunk.
Sheila stutters, stalls.

I jump out
expecting Sheila to be stuck
on a mother-of-a-pine root.
Not a root—
a red-hatted gnome.
Kissing the dirt.

"What'd you do to Winston?"
A girl's voice.
Not the Park President.
But her tone is a combo of peeved principal
and I-want-candy-at-the-checkout toddler.
And then I see her face.
It's Avis's girlfriend.
From Pete's.

She marches over,
picks up Winston, the dumb-named gnome,
and glares with freaky, cucumber-green eyes.
"You could've decapitated him."

"He's got his head.
He shouldn't be hanging out in the road."
My words sound
meaner than I intend.

Pops crooks a wiry eyebrow,
and mouths, "*be nice*."

The girl does a one-eighty arm sweep.
"This isn't a road—
Hey!
It's Mr. Handsome."
She's talking to Avis
who hops out of the golf cart
and crosses over to the dark side.

"Is your tummy all better?"
Avis's girlfriend rubs his belly.

I remember she witnessed
Avis vomit
and my slide of shame.
My face warms to furnace-blast.
I'm in danger of being detonated
by a stray heat-seeking missile.
Might not be a bad thing.

"Time for dinner, Avis."
His favorite words,

to get him back
where he belongs.
Not even an ear twitch.

"Good to meet you, Avis.
I'm Fey."
She smooths his ears.

His eyes roll back into his skull.

Pops whispers, "You could mention your name."

"I'm Hertz."
Which comes out
in a Chewbacca-garbled grunt.

Introducing Trailer 13

After Fey and Avis say their good-byes
we finally land at Trailer 13.

I'm so ready for a couch and
at last,
I'll get my eyes
on a screen.
Any screen.

One step inside Wally Byam's magnificent Airstream
and my dreams crumble like a stomped-on bag of pretzels.

It's a bathroom-sized area
pretending to be a living room with
two brown chairs on metal poles
stuck into lime green carpet.
Brown and yellow curtains—
which must've been
some Scottish dude's kilt—
cover a rounded window.
Underneath,
a bench with the same kilty fabric
imagines itself to be a couch.

Avis, lying under the trailer
outside,
has the roomiest spot.

I will not give up.
"So where did this Wally Byam guy hide the TV?"

"No TV here," Pops says.
"There's one in the communal Friendship Hall.
No cable or satellite or Wi-Fi,
but it plays DVDs."

"Noooooooooooooooooooooo."

A Flippin' Flip Phone

"We better call your mom,
let her know we're here,"
Pops says.
"Just let me find my phone."

Fin-a-lly,
some freakin' technology.
I'm so ready.

Pops pulls out a flippin' flip phone.

I crash onto the mini-couch,
bury my face in kilty plaid.
All hope, dead.

Pops opens and closes
small cupboards
and tiny drawers—
seemingly searching.
"Can't find
Phoebe's cord."

"Who's Phoebe?
Your blender?" I ask.

Pops grins and guffaws.
"Nope, no blender.
Phoebe's the phone."

Of course it is.

He rummages in a
skinny cupboard.
"This will be better anyway."
He slaps down a
hard-sided briefcase.
"You can send your mom
a postcard."

Pine Tree Postcard

Native to **Arizona**, the **Ponderosa pine**.
Scientific Name: ***Pinus ponderosa*** var. ***scopulorum***.

Dear Mom,

Landed at Ponderosa Pines.
No computer, no TV, no phone.
Just trees.
Lots and lots of pines.
Avis likes them.
I like Sheila.
Not a girl—a golf cart.
Miss you lots.

Hertz and Avis

Fire

Snakes of red, yellow, orange slither
across the trailer floor.
Their fiery flaming tongues lick my sheets.

I roll
and get wrapped, trapped
burrito-style.
The pillow bursts into a sparking inferno.

I scream.
There's no sound,
except
the swoooooosh of blood in my ears and
panting.

Avis?

He bounds through the flames,
grabs my blanket in his teeth,
tugs,
setting me free.

But now, we're both
gonna die.

A volcano of flame
erupts,
spits through
the tin-can metal roof.
For a nanosecond
a blue sky and cotton-ball clouds appear, but

thick smoke steals the view.
My throat closes around the red-hot stench.

Avis pulls at my boxers.

I swat his wet nose.

He licks my hand,
my cheek,
my nose.

I wipe dog-drool.
Open. My. Eyes.

No snake flames.
No smoke volcano.
No hole to the sky.

And then I remember—
no technology.
A horrific nightmare.

Show Low Cash and Carry

After breakfast,
Pops steers Cadillac Anastasia through town,
through an open chain-link gate.
He waves hands wide.
"This is a lumberyard."
His voice sounds like the guy on the History Channel
when they open some fossilized dead guy's tomb.

Except here there's nothing
but
rows and rows and rows
of long pieces of wood
stacked taller than
Coach Braziel, our PE teacher
who once played basketball
for the Arizona Wildcats.

"Can't you just see the possibilities?"
Pops's voice still has that what-a-spectacular-discovery tone.
"And there, past the fence,
the back of Pete's Place."

I remember.
Home of the Best Pancake Sundae
and my epically embarrassing
dog-vomit slide.

Pops walks through the stacks
faster than Ben
heading to the cafeteria
when it's Fry It Up Friday.

My bestie, Ben.
Bet he's wearing
VR goggles—
mashing monsters,
annihilating aliens,
crushing Krakens,
at gaming camp.
Not stuck in tool-time torture.

I run to catch up to Pops.

He spouts some kind of code.
"Two-by-four pine.
One-by-six poplar.
Four-by-four pressure-treated."

All I know is
there are enough tree parts
to give the Lorax heart failure.

We walk through a back door,
into a store that
stinks
of locker room mixed with gas station and
lit
with artificial brightness
illuminating
aisles of b-o-r-i-n-g.

A guy with a crazy-shaggy mustache waves.
"Pops. How are you?"

"Doing fine, Carlos. This is Hertz, my great-nephew."

Carlos grins, showing bits of white teeth under
his awesome 'stache,
which is long enough to gel and twirl the ends
into villain curls.

I smooth the fuzz under my nose.
One day.

Carlos pulls an end of his 'stache.
"My kid Allen's around.
Likely in my office
on the computer."

My heart trips, flops, skids.
Bright blasts of
YouTube,
Goblin Gitmo,
Candy Bombs
flash.

Pops tugs my arm.
"First, I want to give you the full tour of
Show Low Cash and Carry."

My temporary techno bubble of possibility bursts.

I'm Not a Firebug

Down a mind-numbing aisle
Pops stops in front of open bins,
and hands me a paper bag.

"Grab a handful—those there."
Pops taps a bin.

I reach in.
Pointy nails bite.
I grit my teeth,
close my hand around
a thousand stinging bees,
pull out a nest of nails.

"Glad I found you."
A voice I know.
Sheriff Show Low.
The cop who stopped
when Anastasia broke down.
The cop who wanted to take
Avis to the shelter.

He stands at the end of the aisle
in a Superman pose.
Legs wide, arms crossed over his
puffed up chest.
Faint scent of smoke oozes.
Not fresh-from-a-fire smoke.
More like barbecue-sauce smoke.

Pops wraps an arm around my shoulders.

"Hello, Sheriff.
You in need of some nuts and bolts?"

"Not the kind of nut I'm looking for."
Sheriff Show Low fires me a loaded look.
And he's not shooting Nerf darts.
He's using big gauge ammo.
"I'm looking for the nut who set fire
to the recycling bin at Ponderosa Pines.
Someone like the Phoenix Firebug."

Friendship Bin

"I heard the bin behind Friendship Hall
caught fire," Pops says.
"Didn't hear anything about it
being intentionally set.
Most likely an accident.
Could be something as simple as
a cigarette butt thrown in by mistake."
His words have a sure-bet tone.

I straighten my shoulders,
squint my eyes, and aim
asteroids-of-death
at Sheriff Show Low.

Sheriff's not fizzled or frazzled.
"The bin melted.
Contents are mostly ash.
Gonna be hard to tell whether it was
accidental or intentional.
Hertzog, do you smoke?"

"No way."
My hands shake,
the nails I'm clutching drop,
scatter,
ping and pong,
like Skittles at a movie theater,
creating a minefield between
Sheriff Show Low and me.

"Play with matches then?" Sheriff says.

"Most boys play with matches at some time.
Caught my son at about your age.
Or a lighter?"
Sheriff nods as if
by dipping his triple-decker chin
I'm going to agree.

"Sheriff, sounds like you're interrogating
my great-nephew." Pops's voice is low,
controlled,
but with a back-off warning.
Makes me proud we share some DNA.

"There's your great-nephew's
arson history in Phoenix.
All over the internet."
Sheriff Show Low says this like
that's all the evidence he needs
to lock me up.

"Stop. Right. There."
Pops kicks aside some nails
steps in front,
protecting
me.
"You're making a huge leap from
an accident in Phoenix
to arson in Show Low."
He turns his back on the sheriff,
looks me in the eyes.
And I know—
he knows
I didn't set any fire in a bin.
"Come on, Hertz.

This store has suddenly lost its appeal."

"No need to leave on my account,"
Sheriff Show Low says.
"But there sure better not be any more fires
in Show Low while you're in town
Hertzog Zindler."

Fantastic.
Won't Mom be proud.
Twenty-four hours
and I'm top of Sheriff Show Low's
arson hit list.

No Tech Commiseration

Sheriff Show Low swaggers to the exit.

Pops goes in search of Carlos for lumber.

I'm still standing in the nail-aisle when…

"You play ball?" The voice comes from a mini-Carlos.
Except no mustache.
Must be his kid, Allen.

"Only ball I play is *Jeter's Cheaters,*" I say.

"Me too. My fantasy team
went all the way to the World Series.
We should play sometime."

At the mention of actually playing
a video game
I do a happy dance
and stub my toe on
a display of chain saws.
Ooooooow-ch.

"You'll likely lose your toenail," Allen says.

"Just add it to the growing list
of things I've lost," I say.
"Gaming camp, computer, TV, phone—"

"No phone." Allen slams his soda can
on a skid of ant-killer.

"Not you, too?
I got three weeks.
No phone, no computer, no TV.
All because Mom found a cigarette butt
in the toilet.
My brother wouldn't fess up
and I'm no snitch."
Allen's words spill over like his fizzy soda.

All I hear is my
dreams of sharing screens
with this kid getting flushed.

"What's there to do around here?" I ask.

"You mean here? As in the store? Or the town?"

I glance at the b-o-r-i-n-g aisles.
"The town."

Allen pulls a crumpled paper from his pocket.
"This could be cool.
Chamber of Commerce Scavenger Hunt.
First prize—five hundred bucks."

$500 = a new tablet or laptop or phone or game console or...

Techno jingles play in my winner-takes-all brain.

Frog Farts

"Hey, Hex Head." The voice is from a taller version of Allen.

"Why are you and the Frog Farts here, Weasel?"
Allen asks.

"What'd you say, Slug Slime?"
Brilliant comeback from
the blonde guy
behind Allen's brother.
I recognize him and the other skinny dude.
Jordan and Matt.
They messed with me at Pete's
after my dog vomit skid.
These guys have ammunition
to trash-talk me for twenty years.

"Since when did you become friends with Puke Pants?"
Jordan swings his diss my way.
"He come to teach you the dog-barf slide?
With a cherry on the crotch?"
He fist-bumps Matt.

Confusion floats over Allen's face.
"Barfing dog?
You mean
like when you spewed your cookies
in the back shed
after you
smoked Dad's cigars?"

"Shut. Up," Allen's brother says.

"You said you'd keep quiet."

"I said I won't tell.
And you said
you and the Frog Farts would leave me alone.
That goes for my friend too.
So back off."

I'm stun-gunned surprised.
Allen's tough and he called me his friend,
and I didn't even save virtual butt
in *Comrade in Arms*.

Mouthy Jordan's Not Done

Jordan zeroes in,
"Did you know, Puke Pants is
a Phoenix celebrity?
Went viral for
setting his own house on fire."
Jordan's eyes have a villain glint,
but his tone holds a hint
of something else.
Something like admiration.

"Who cares?"
Matt says.

"My dad cares.
My dad,
the sheriff,"
Jordan says.

Figures,
in a town the size of a tick's toenail,
mouthy Jordan would be
Sheriff Show Low's son.
And he's not done.

"I let Dad know about our viral visiting celebrity.
And then there was that blaze.
Right where pyro-boy sleeps."

"Since when did you become daddy's little deputy?"
Allen says.

"Better be careful around here, Firebug.
One spark and
all this wood
would be an epic inferno."
Matt's words don't sound like a warning,
they sound like a dare.

Need Three for a Team

Allen stood up
for me,
talked down the Frog Farts
for me.
Called me
his friend.

So, when he tells me
we need at least three
for the scavenger hunt,
I figure
I owe him.
Now Avis and I are
back at Ponderosa Pines behind
Friendship Hall
looking for Fey.

The fire-breathing dragon
on Fey's t-shirt glows in the dark.
She tosses something in the
garbage bin.
Was it glowing?
No. Just Sheriff Show Low haunting me.

"Hey, handsome."
She's talking to Avis.
She pets his head.

His dopey eyes roll back.
He's in love.

Fey checks out Sheila,
the golf cart.
"Can you drive me over to Mrs. Mason?
I'm to bring her leftovers from the
potluck."

"Sure." Maybe I can impress Fey
with my super-stellar driving skills.

Fey sits, slaps the dash.
"Let's roll."
Avis lays at her feet.

"Which trailer is Mrs. Mason's?" I ask.

"She doesn't live in the park."

"Um. I'm not sure…"
The inside of my mouth feels like
I just chewed a handful of Ritz crackers.

"Don't fret it. Mrs. Mason lives
just past the gate."

I swallow and follow
Fey's directions,
through the park gate.
Then stop.

Fear rears
and kicks
my confidence to Saturn.

Golf Cart Suicide

"We can get real speed
down this hill."
Fey's words fly into the night
like bats leaving a cave.

I stare dead ahead.
This isn't a hill.
It's golf cart suicide
s
 t
  e
  e
   p.

A hundred yards of
gnarly gravel.

At the end,
the ramp-of-death,
a paved intersection where
real cars whiz.

I white-knuckle
the steering wheel
and check.
No seat belt.
No airbag.
No parachute.

"What are you waiting for?" Fey asks.

I can do this.
I've been driving since noon.
And I cannot add
colossal wimp
to my already stellar resume
of embarrassment in front of Fey.

"I'm ready," I say.
"But in case we die,
would you consider being on
a scavenger hunt team with me?"

Fey braces her hands on the dash.
"You do this hill and I'm in."

Sheila starts off slow and steady,
staying on the hard-packed tracks.
I'm in command,
in control,
definitely cool.

Then we pick up speed.
Faster, faster, fa-a-a-a-a-a-st-er.

My heart ba-booms,
like during the last lap of
the mile run in PE.
I lift my foot from the gas.

Fey grabs my knee.
"Don't you dare brake."

I don't dare.

We fly down the ramp-of-death.

Fey throws her arms in the air
like on a roller coaster.
"Whooo hooooooo."

The paved road and whizzing cars loom.
C l o s e r, c l o s e r, closer.

The blood pounds in my ears
and orders
brake, brake, brake.

I do
and
we bounce, bounce, bounce.

Hit a ditch,
rocket into the air.

"Whoaaaaaa…" Fey's voice fades.

Sheila lands.

I look beside me.
No Fey.

Avis leaps out, barks.

Fey pops up from long grass, laughs.

No fairy twitter giggle.
Her laugh is one big blast,
like bowling pins hit with a strike.

"For the love of dragon spit," she says.
"I'll be on your team."

Quail Postcard

The scaled **quail** is found primarily in the open country of
eastern **Arizona.**
Scientific Name: **Callipepla squamata**

Dear Mom,

Not much new in Dullsville, AZ.
Drove Sheila down Suicide Hill.
Avis and I didn't die.
Neither did Fey or Sheila.
Pops and I cooked
cookies and the
best chicken ever!
Only three ingredients—
chicken, can of Coke, and a cup of ketchup.

Miss you,
Hertz and Avis

Leaky Valve

Too early for
stirring,
slurping,
and
whistling.

Through squinty
not-awake-yet eyes
I see Pops grinning.
Rodent eyebrows waggling,
he holds a
cup of steaming
something.
"Rise and shine.
Gotta get a move on.
Gloria's got a
leaky valve and
I could use
your skillfulness."

I mash fists
into my eyes
and rub.
"I don't have any
valve skills.
I don't even
know what a
valve is."

"Oh, but you do.
You'll see."

After four
toaster waffles
smeared with
honey,
Avis and I climb
aboard
Sheila.
Pops insists
I drive.

Sheila whirs
and Pops begins
a lesson
on valves.
"The valve
is a truly marvelous device."

This can't go quick enough.
I step on the gas.

Pops's pitch rises with wonder.
"A valve is
any moveable part
that opens, shuts, or
partially obstructs
flow."
He spreads his arms wide.
"And valves are everywhere."

"Everywhere?"

"Yes. Turn left.
Stop at
Friendship Hall,

I'll show you a
valve."

"But I thought
we were fixing a
valve at Gloria's."

"We are. But
you'll love this valve."

Me?
Loving a valve?
Sounds like a
vast desert-sized stretch.

Gummy Valve

Inside Friendship Hall,
next to the karaoke machine,
standing four feet tall,
perches an old-fashioned
gumball machine.

"Ta-da." Pops pulls out a quarter.
"Go ahead. Use the valve."
He points at the shiny,
chrome turning-handle below
the big round ball of glass
filled with colorful jawbreakers.

I slip the
quarter in the slot,
turn the handle.
Plop.
A giant red one
slides onto my palm.

"There you go," Pops says,
satisfied.
"Turning the handle
activated a valve."

I suck on the jawbreaker.
Sweeeeeeeet
tangy
cherry.

Pops was right.

I might actually love this valve.

Go With the Flow

We arrive at Trailer 9.
I recognize the red-hatted Gnome.
Same trailer Fey's staying at.
I almost choke on the jawbreaker.

The smart part of me
hopes Fey's not here.
The idiot part
hopes she is.

Pops is at the door,
toolbox-ready.
"Let's go.
I really will need your
expertise."

My knees quake and shake
but I make it inside.
Same decor as Pops's trailer,
except instead of kilty-fabric—
big yellow flowers.

I scan, sniff, search for Fey.
Turns out she's not here.
Turns out Gloria is Fey's grandma.
Turns out my skill is
small shoulders,
small hands,
small fingers.

I wiggle

into the cabinet under the sink.

"You've got the skill," Pops says.
"Use this adjustable crescent wrench to
remove the cold-water compression fittings."

Yeah, right.

Pops instructs.
I get splashed on the head,
removing the fittings.
Knock my elbow on the drainpipe,
installing the new pipe.
And then
hurt my face,
smiling wide when
I open the valve,
turn on the water,
and no leak.

Pops slaps me on the back.
"Valve expert."

No Control in Show Low

Another daylight dawns
in Tech-Zero World.
Riding shotgun
in Anastasia—
Pops's tricked-out tribute
to the American flag.
He should've named her Betsy Ross.

Cool leather against my back,
red carpet under my feet,
through the windshield
a stretch of gravel leading to
my inevitable nuclear explosion of embarrassment.

No way I'm gonna survive
a live,
in-person,
scavenger hunt.

Why couldn't this hunt have been online?
Not that I have any way to get online.

How I miss the cool grip
of a hard plastic game controller
where I could control the universe.

I have no control in Show Low
and all my hands hold,
a paper bag stuffed with cookies.

I scrunch and un-scrunch

the top of the bag.

"Careful, or you'll end up with
crumbs, not cookies," Pops says.
"Your friends are gonna love
our peanut butter snickerdoodles."

Pops says *friends* as if I have some.
I think he's wrong.

Despite my rocket golf-cart ride with Fey,
I'm terrified
she'll learn
I'm not brave,
not confident,
not cool.
I definitely braked
on Suicide Hill.
I'm a fraud.

Arizona Legend

Pops takes a left onto *Deuce of Clubs*,
the town's main street.
"There's the Chamber of Commerce. Up on the right."

A brown building looks like a saloon
in Old West movies.
There's a sign—
Show Low Chamber of Commerce,
a two of clubs playing card
on either side of the words.

Pops stops at a red light.
"You know how this road and
the town got their names?"

I don't answer.
My stare stuck on the crowd
in front of the Chamber.
My palms drippy-popsicle sticky.

"An Arizona legend."
I sense Pops is primed
for a story filled
with more trivia
than *Jeopardy's Tournament of Champions.*

"A marathon card game between two guys,
Cooley and Clark
who despised each other.
But instead of drawing pistols,
they drew poker cards.

Whoever got the lower card
showed low
and would win.
Winner'd get to stay,
even name the town.
Loser had to leave."
Pops's voice is all
I-won-the-lottery excited.
"Cooley drew a deuce of clubs.
Lowest possible draw and
named the town Show Low.
Get it?"

The light turns green,
dread drips into my veins.
The light was too short.
The story too fast.

Chamber of Annihilation

Pops parks in front of
the Chamber of My Annihilation.
(Show Low's Chamber of Commerce.)
On the sidewalk,
Jordan and Matt.
The Dark Angels of Humiliation.
They look,
point,
laugh,
lean over,
and pretend-puke.

I duck. "Go, go, go, go, go."

Confusion twists Pops's wrinkles
into question marks.
"I thought you were—"

"Yeah, yeah. Just don't park here.
Pleeeeeease."
My whine works.

Pops steps on the gas.
We shoot from the curb.
He takes a right,
goes half a block,
and then parks
at the back of the Chamber.

"This parking place work for you?"
No anger tints his words.

Just a twitchy smile.
I'm not sure what to say.
Pops wouldn't get it.
He's sure about everything.
From thermostats to Cadillacs to valves.

"I get it," he says.
"You want a low-key entrance.
Anastasia might be too much.
Or maybe it's my shirt?"
His shirt has kangaroos holding
tiny American flags
hopping across his chest.

I catch myself grinning.
"It's not the car. Or your shirt."

Pops wears his I've-got-all-day expression.
"I saw Fey back there—
Allen too—
waiting for their team captain."

"Me?"

"Sure. Why not?"

Grandmas and Girlfriends

No excuses,
no options,
me and the bag of cookies
head to the back of the Chamber building
in July's asteroid heat.

"You made it." Allen darts from behind
the Chamber's dented dumpster.
He scares me so bad
I almost drop the cookies
and a load in my shorts.

Allen leads the way,
talking, talking, talking.

At the front of the building
a pumped-up crowd mingles.
A team of three guys wear shirts
printed with *Sam's Seniors*.
High school cheerleaders in matching pleated skirts
huddle,
their thumbs fly over their phones.
I drool
over the phones.

Allen slides us in beside a team of grandmas
in purple t-shirts and red hats.
"Soooooo, where's your girlfriend?" Allen asks.

"You've got a girlfriend?"
Fey says from behind the grandmas.

Weird, wimpy feelings scorch my cheeks.

Fey doesn't notice.
She bounces a hacky sack
from one scraped knee to the other.
She's wearing a Smokey the Bear t-shirt
with the words
Fire Danger Very High.
She looks at Allen.
"I'm Fey. And I'm nobody's girlfriend."

Scavenger Hunt Clue Number One

Allen leaps

       off

          the Chamber's

              steps,

                   "Got the clues."

Fey plucks
the list.

Allen twitches.
"Come on. Come on. Read it."

"Are you always this jacked?" Fey asks.
"Or did you shower in Red Bull?"

"I didn't, but
maybe you should've,"
Allen shoots back.

Fey puffs up tall.
"Rules say
no using phones,
computers,
or GPS."

Allen slaps his pockets.
"Got nothing.

How about you, Hertz?
Anything in your bag?"

"Just cookies," I say.

Fey jabs the paper.
"Listen up."
She sounds like Mrs. Connelly,
my English teacher,
about to explain a standardized test.
"First clue,
What's on the menu for the early bird?"

Fey and Allen buzz and bicker.

I force my brain out of
summer vacation
hibernation.
BOOM.
One of Pops's oldster sayings
detonates.
"The early bird catches the worm," I say.

Allen bounces.
"Good. We need worms. Where?
Do we dig for 'em?"

"No, it says…" Fey reads,
"Ten items are to be collected
from ten different
Chamber of Commerce businesses."

"What's a chamber business?" I ask.
"Something to do with the Chamber of Secrets?"

I'm hoping to add funny so Allen and Fey
will work together,
not argue.

"No *Harry Potter* stuff," Allen says,
no hint of a smile.
"My dad's lumberyard belongs to
the Chamber.
So do most of the small businesses
in town."

"Okay, then we need a business
that has worms," I say,
getting us back to the business
of solving the riddle.

"Bob's Bait and Tackle."
Allen blasts this news
loud enough for teams on Jupiter to hear.

"Right. Birdseed. Ellen's Pet Emporium,"
Fey says,
then takes off running.

I sprint after Fey.
"I thought we were after worms?"

"I'm throwing off
the other teams," she says.

Allen flies by.
"Smart move.
Next left.
Shortcut to Bob's."

Fishing in Alaska

A garbage-filled alley,
another left,
and we land at
Bob's Bait and Tackle.

Behind the counter
there's a skinny guy
with a scruffy beard
and a cap with "Fish Fear Me."

Allen doesn't fear anyone.
"Give us a worm,"
he says all throaty and tough.

"Don't sell *one* worm.
You gotta buy a dozen,"
Scruffy Beard says.

Allen turns to Fey.
"Are we supposed to buy
these things?"

"It says nothing about buying.
Says the Chamber member will present—"

"Hold on." Scruffy Beard pushes back his cap.
"You talking about the Chamber of Commerce?
They sending kids now?
I told the lady last week
Bob is fishing
in Alaska.

I can't authorize any
Chamber membership."

"You're not a Chamber member?
You're not part of the scavenger hunt?"
Allen's voice loses all gruffness.

"Don't know anything about a hunt," Scruffy Beard says.
"You can get free worms
in the dirt.
Go dig 'em up."

Allen squirms, as if
he's ready to dig for worms
in Scruffy's beard.

I pull Allen's shirt.
"He's right. Worms live in dirt.
How about a nursery?"

"What do babies
have to do with worms?" Allen asks.

"Not that nursery, genius.
A garden store—with flowers."
Fey walks out.

"I know a place."
Allen's through the door
faster than Sonic the Hedgehog.

"Sorry we bothered you, sir."
I hold out my paper bag.
"How about a cookie?"

Scruffy takes one.

"Good luck finding your worm."

Roses Not Worms

Running through a deserted park,
back onto Deuce of Clubs,
and into Mary June's Florals.

A woman in a green apron
cuts the end off a red rose
with a pair of monster-sized scissors.

"Worm."
The word spurts from Allen's mouth
like a spit-wad.

Fey fires Allen an evil-sorceress glare.
"Ma'am, are you a Chamber member?"

Apron Lady points her shears
at a framed Chamber certificate.

Fey continues,
"We're part of the Chamber of Commerce
Scavenger hunt and—"

"We need a worm," Allen says.
"Do you have a worm?
You must.
You got plenty of plants.
In dirt.
Worms live in dirt.
Where's the worm?"
Allen hammers the words
like a detective grilling a suspect.

Apron Lady aims her shears,
pointy-end at Allen.
"You need to slow down."

Worried she might snip off Allen's nose,
I say,
"We're on a scavenger hunt.
Maybe you heard about it at the last Chamber meeting?"
I'm using my charm-my-way-out-of-detention voice.
Not sure why.
It never works.

Apron Lady shakes her head.
"I don't go to the meetings."

"But do you have a worm?"
Allen leans over the counter
as if he expects a jar of
wriggling night crawlers
to be sitting at Apron Lady's feet.

She waves her shears.
"Get off my counter.
And unless one of you is buying something,
you'd better leave."

"Sorry, ma'am."
I stretch out the crumpled snack bag.
"Maybe you'd like a cookie?"

Letter B Brainwave

Outside, Fey pulls out the clue sheet.
"We must be missing something.
Item one:
What's on the menu for the early bird?"

Nothing new.
I keep my mouth shut.

Not Allen.
"Has to be a worm. Birds eat worms."

"Birds eat lots of things.
Bugs. Berries. Birdseed."
Fey bounces her hacky sack off
      elbow,

                knee,

   foot.

"No playtime. Solve-the-clue time."
Allen swipes
at the hacky sack,
but misses.

"This helps me think," Fey says.
Thwap. Thwap. Thwap.
She spins,
tips
  her
    head,
catches the sack.

On.
Her.
Ear.
"I've got it," she says.
We need to find something that starts with
the letter B. Like bugs, berries, birdseed."

The hacky sack must've
smacked, whacked
her brain cells.
Nothing in the clue
about the letter B.

"Hel-looo." Allen waves both hands.
"Bob's Bait and Tackle.
Two Bs in the name."

Fey's letter B brainwave has
as much chance as a
hurricane in Arizona.
But I don't say anything
because
1. she'll think I'm a turd troll.
2. I need to keep our team together
not split us even more.

"Let's skip this clue."
Allen's hopping foot-to-foot.

"We can't skip it."
Fey reads,
"*Items must be gathered in order.*
Once an item is located,
you must present the item

to the next business and collect a code.
You cannot skip items."

More blah-blah.

My mind's searching
for a link
to *early bird*.
My fingers itch for a
phone,
keyboard,
Wi-Fi,
Google.

Then my brain,
all on its own,
gets a HIT.
"Pete's Pancakes.
Early bird special."

"Hertz, you're brilliant. I've seen the Chamber plaque
on Pete's wall."

Allen's off.

For the sake of my aching legs,
I sure hope this time I'm right.

Choking on Bits of Lung

We dart
across parking lots,
around buildings,
through another smelly alley,
and jay-walk
twice.

We spy other teams,
coming,
going,
looping,
in lost circles
like us.

I will not be
a slacker couch-potato
in front of Fey.

My lungs burn.
My legs burn.
My smushed toenail burns.

We skirt the back fence
of the lumberyard.
Does Allen know where he's going?
Isn't Pete's blocks away?

I'm choking on
bits of lung,
but it will be worth it
when we finally

get the clue.

We squeeze through a fence hole,
pound across gravel—
there's a white building,
back door open,
smell of pancakes.

We stampede through
and slam-stop
under the Cadillac-hood-sized chalkboard.
Panting and puffing like the Big Bad Wolf's
out-of-shape cousin,
I drip sweat.

Francis whisks batter.
Pete pours coffee.

At the counter,
Sheriff Show Low
shoots me a death-scowl.

Throwing Allen Under the Bus

My stomach flips.
Like a pancake.

"Another fire was just reported,"
Sheriff Show Low says.
"Behind the Chamber of Commerce.
In their dumpster."
The words ricochet off the walls
of the almost-full diner.
"When I investigate,
will I find you were there today
Hertzog Zindler?"

Pete stops pouring.
Francis stops whisking.
I stop breathing.

A lump bigger and drier than a day-old donut
sticks in my throat.
I choke down sour spit.
And from a deep, dark, dumb place
I decide to speak.
"I did walk by the dumpster,
but I didn't start a fire.
Could've been anyone.
Anyone doing the scavenger hunt.
The Frog Farts.
Sam's Seniors.
The Red Hats.
Allen—"

"Hey. Not cool." Allen whacks my arm.

Pete stashes the coffee.
"Kids. Outside. Now."

Another Super-Sized Screw Up

Out back,
no more sweet breakfast smells,
just the stench of
my latest and greatest
super-sized screw-up.

I knew the words were
wrong, bad, stupid
the second they
spilled from my lips.

Pete's frown makes
my nerves jitter,
my skin itch.
I fear I'll melt
into a puddle of goo.

"Did any of you
have anything to do
with the fire at the Chamber?"
Pete asks.

Heads shake,
but Fey and Allen
don't look at me.

"Good."
Pete hands me a folded paper.
"Your first clue.
My Early Bird Menu."

Allen rips the menu
from my quivery fingers.
Throws me a glare of glass shards,
stalks off.

Fey's flat stare hits me
like a bucket of mud.

Pete says, "Don't know what's up
with you and the sheriff, but
you shouldn't talk to him without Pops.
And you should definitely avoid
throwing your friends
under the sheriff-suspect bus.
You're a team."

I watch Allen and Fey hanging together
by the fence,
reading the clue sheet
behind a wall of wrath.

"They don't want me," I say.
"Bet they think I am the one
starting the fires."

"Are you?" Pete asks.

"No."

"So don't give up on your team.
Apologize.
Make a case for
why they need you."

I grab onto the Penny-of-Dumb
and edge over
to ladle out an apology.

Super-Sorry Snacks

"I'm sorry.
Really sorry.
I'm stupid,
with a stupider mouth.
There's no reason
you should want me on the team except…
I know we can do this.
We can win."
I offer up my
I'm-so-sorry snacks.
"How about a cookie?"

Allen notches back his glare from
I-should-strangle-you to
I-could-slap-you.
He takes a cookie,
stuffs it in his mouth.
"Apology accepted and
so far you haven't been
the most horrible clue-solver.
That title goes to Fey."

"Hey." Fey shoves Allen
and takes a peace-offering-cookie.
"You guys would be nowhere
without me.
Next clue is
What helps you take a bite out of life?"

Allen folds into the spring of the chain-link fence.
"These clues are crazy cryptic.

You need teeth to bite.
Think we need a tooth?"

"Where d'we get a tooth?
Kidnap the Tooth Fairy?"
Fey's voice is tinged with snark.

"Yeah. I'll call the Easter Bunny to help."
Allen doubles the nasty.

"Remember, we need Chamber members."
I do my best
teacher-settle-down impression.

"Dentist," Allen says.
And he's off.

Hard to believe I'm voluntarily running
to a dentist.

Suicide Crossing

"For the love of dragon spit,
it's closed."
Fey slaps a sign on the window.

"Forget the dentist," Allen says.
"Across the street.
Farley's Pharmacy is a Chamber member.
They have a whole aisle of tooth things."

Deuce of Clubs is four lanes of
gas-powered,
hurtling hunks of metal.
Doesn't stop Allen.
He dodges cars like
he's Donkey Kong.

Miraculously, he crosses two lanes,
but he's stuck straddling
the middle yellow line.

Fey heads to the traffic light.
"The sugar's messed with Allen's head.
I'm not joining his suicide mission."

I scour the rushing river of cars,
and spot a cop car.
Stomach drops to the curb.

Likely Sheriff Show Low
looking to nab me for
jay walking,

or arson,
or an unsolved murder.

But there's Allen.
Definitely jaywalking.
"Allen! Cops!"

He threads between truck and van.
Horn blasts.
Fey shrieks,
grabs my hand.
My heart slams.
Stalls.

A minivan passes,
Allen grins from the
far side of Deuce of Clubs.

Heart reboots.

My sweaty Elmer's Glue palm tingles,
warm
against Fey's
cool.
I haven't touched a girl's hand
since third grade gym class
when Coach Mendez made us
do sing-songy square dances.
And I'm not letting go.

I float along the block until...
at the corner—
there's Jordan and Matt.

I crash land in reality,
and pull Fey behind a parked pick-up,
scrunch low.
"Other teams.
Can't give away Farley's."

She frowns,
but ducks.

I sneak a peek—
fifty feet between us
and Matt and Jordan
and Sheriff Show Low's cruiser.
Pulse panicking.

Fey dashes,
me in tow,
hand-in-hand.

Another miracle.
We crossed Deuce of Clubs.

Allen greets us,
looks at us holding hands,
"You two an item now?"

I like his thinking.

Farley's Pharmacy

Tons of teams crowd the
dental supply aisle—
snatch brushes,
floss, picks, paste.

At the register
are the cheerleaders.
Cashier Connie hands
back a toothbrush,
"Right place.
Wrong item."

Back to the tooth aisle they go.
Teams huddle—
confer over the clue.

Fey whispers in Allen's ear.

Jealousy squirms
in my chest.

I'll find the clue.
I'll be the hero.

I scan endless floss—
waxed, unwaxed, tape, thread,
cinnamon, mint, picks,
then
a blue box with a
white-haired guy
eating an apple.

Big words.
"Denture Glue Can Help You
Take a Bite Out of Life."
Got to be Clue Number Two.

Clue Number Three

High-fives
and "way-to-go, Hertz"–es
puff me up.

I float
like a balloon
over Deuce of Clubs.

"Hertz, pay attention."
Fey pops my
pride-bubble.
"Clue number three,
Use this rather than your mama's spit."

"Napkin," says Allen.

"Tissue," says Fey.

"What?" I say.

"Doesn't your mom wipe gunk off your face
with her spit?" Allen asks.

"My mom doesn't see gunk on my face.
She doesn't see."
Missing-mom feelings twist.
Two phone calls and
the postcards
doesn't seem enough.

Fey and Allen squawk

and caw like crows in
a cornfield.

"What about the *mama* word," I say.
"I never call my mom *Mama*."

"Mama's Pizzeria," they say
in a creepy-connected way.

Inside Mama's
we pick up a napkin
and trade our denture glue
for another code.

"Hertz, you're a clue-solving whiz,"
Allen says.

"We're on fire," Fey says.

Crushing the Clues

We tornado through clue four.
A Cup with Joe.
A paper cup
signed by coffee shop owner, Joe.
Joe samples my cookies.

Clue five:
Never keep your dough under the mattress.
A blank deposit slip from
Show Low Savings and Loan.

Clue six and seven
are two more banks.
A credit card application
from the Bank of Central Arizona.
A dog biscuit from
the drive-thru window of
White Mountain Credit Union.
Avis would munch out on
that clue.
Lots of banks belong to
the Chamber of Commerce.

Clue eight, not a bank
but Allen knows
the chips you'd never eat
are paint chip samples
and his dad says we're the
first team to Show Low Cash and Carry.

Heart racing,

pumped to win
my tech-less days
soon to be over.

Clue Number Nine

Losing your locks?
Three inches will save the day.

Fey and Allen squabble
still in the aisles of Show Low Cash and Carry.
Combination locks, padlocks, keys.

"The locks can't be here,"
I remind them.
"We need a different business.
Another kind of locks."

Allen plows
out the door.

Fey and I run.

Fey and Allen bicker
back and forth.

"George's," says Allen.

"Casey's," says Fey.

I have no idea who, what, or where—
I just keep running.

We swerve around
garbage cans,
lampposts,
fire hydrants.

"George's."

"Casey's."

George's

A red, white, and blue
barbershop pole
marks the entrance.
Inside it reeks of
aftershave.
Chrome and red vinyl
barber chairs line up
in front of a big mirror.

Allen dives,
crawls,
scoops
hair clippings
off the floor.

"Allen Delgado.
Get off my floor,"
says a bushy-bearded guy with
a straight-edge razor,
and George stitched
on his white jacket.

Allen snakes, slithers, stealing hair.

The guy in a chair,
beard of foam says,
"You after my DNA?
No way I'm your daddy.
I'm too old."

Under the window,

perched on plastic chairs,
two guys laugh so hard
their coffee spills.

George pulls
Allen to his feet.
"Put that hair in the garbage."

"Great idea. The garbage."
Allen leaps to the can.

"Don't be digging in my trash."

"But the scavenger hunt.
We need three inches of hair
to save the day."
Allen's voice is amped to
squirrel-chatter.

"You want hair?
Get the broom.
Start sweeping,"
George says.

Allen sends a satisfied smirk to Fey.
"See? Right place.
George just wants us to
use the broom, then
we'll trade him for
the code."

"Don't know a code."
George hands Allen a broom.

"No code?" Allen slumps.

Fey raises an eyebrow
in a throw-down-dare.
"Casey's," she says
and walks to the door.

Allen swings the broom
at Fey's butt.
And for some idiotic,
save-the-damsel-in-distress reason,
I jump
in front of the bristles.

Broom smashes my gut.
I inhale air and hair.
I wheeze and sneeze.

"So-rrrrrry."
Allen pats my back.

"It's okay," I say.
Not really.
But maybe taking the broom-smash
settles the score
for me throwing Allen
under the sheriff-suspect bus.

Problem is
I took the bristle-hit
for Fey.
She didn't even notice.

Casey's Creations

Hair dryers whir,
scissors snip,
women gab.

Holy Wombats—
a wondrous widescreen.

I stare,
hypnotized by
the potent pixels and
a two-foot-high box of cereal
dancing across seventy inches.

A hand waves in my face.
"Stop gawking at the dumb commercial," Fey says.
"You want to win?"

I do.
But I need TV.
Maybe more.

A woman with red hair
and a black smock
steps in front of the TV.
"You have an appointment?
Your mom here?"

I angle my head
around her and catch
details on the Ford Fusion.

"Unless there's someone you know here,
you need to leave."
Smock lady sounds as mean as
the Frankenstein guy searching
for his Buick on the TV commercial.

"Ma'am, we noticed
your Chamber of Commerce sticker."
Fey coats her words in sweet syrup.
"We're searching for a clue."

"I wasn't expecting kids."
She shuts off the TV.

Noooooooooo.

Mad Mom

Allen dives,
grabs clumps of hair
on the tiled floor of Casey's Creations.
"Got it."

Fey squints.
"Doesn't look like three inches
like the clue says."

"Sure it is," Allen says.

"No, it isn't," she says.

"Yes, it is."
Allen shoves the hair in her face,
then holds it out to me.
"Measure."

I pull out
the multi-tool pocketknife
with a mini ruler
Pops gave me.
"Two and a half inches."

Fey waves a wad of hair.
"Try this."

I measure. "Two and three quarters."

Allen jumps on a hairstylist chair.
"Excuse me,

any of you ladies have
three inches of hair cut off today?"
No one speaks.
No one seems to care
about Allen on a chair.

"How about donating
three inches of hair?"
Allen begs.

"Emanuel Allen Delgado.
Get down from there."
A woman in a purple plastic cape,
with tin foil on her head
stalks over.

"Ah, Mom," Allen says,
"I'm just trying to save the day."

"Look, it's Puke Pants
and his team of losers."
This zinger comes from Jordan,
slithering toward us
with his sidekick Matt.

And Allen's older brother.
"What'd you do?
Cry big baby tears
to Mom?
Ask for her help?"
He socks Allen in the shoulder.

Allen punches back.

"I'm calling your father."
Mrs. Delgado's tone
is mad-mom scary.

Fey drags me to a wall
of hair products.
"I figured out the clue.
Like the Denture Glue.
The words are on the package."
She points.
Bold letters on a hairbrush box
claim
Losing your locks?
Three-inch bristles will save the day,

We high-five.
I want to hug,
but only because we've almost won,
and a used laptop will soon be mine.
Not because Fey's smart
and quirky
and kind of cute
and held my hand.

Fey checks her watch.
"Twenty minutes left."

Allen's trapped in a solid mom grip.
He gives a go-go-go wave.

We clue-solver sneak
out of the salon.

The Final Clue

Feed the collected codes
into hungry machines
surrounded by books.

"The library," Fey and I say together.
Which must mean we've crossed
into soulmate territory.

But my soulmate takes off,
running,
down Deuce of Clubs.

A left,
another left,
a short street to
Show Low Public Library.
And the purple shirt grandmas at the entrance.

Oh, total turd toads,
we're not first.

Fey barrels between them,
but one lady stops her.

I drag my sweaty, defeated self over.

Fey's face is chalk-white.
She hands me the hunt codes.
"Go. Gramma Glo fell.
She's okay, but I gotta go."
Her lip quivers.

Crying girls are about as much fun
as getting your immunization shots.
And this is hacky-sacking,
clue-solving,
team-slaying Fey.

"I'll do it," I say.
"And I hope your grandma is okay."
Our team has shrunk to one.
But...

Maybe Pops was right.
Maybe I can be the leader.
Maybe I can save our team.
And now I know—
we can WIN.

Rhinoceros Librarian

Library lady,
older and wrinklier than the
rhino at the Phoenix Zoo,
guards the desk.

"I need a computer," I say.

"You need a library card," she says.

"But I don't have a card."

"Then you don't get a computer."

I give her the Avis look
when I forget to feed him.
Big, sad eyes.
Pouty, down-turned mouth.
The why-are-you-being-so-mean
soft, slack face.
"Pleeeeeeeease."

She looks at me like
I'm a tattooed, pierced, punk rocker
who wants to date
her great-granddaughter.
"As I said, you need a library card."

Defeat pools in my shoes.
I slap the clue sheet on the counter.
"Useless hunt."

"The Chamber Scavenger Hunt?"
Rhino Librarian hands me a clipboard.
"Special sign-in sheet. You can use
terminal twenty-two.
But we close at five."

Trapped in Level One

My fingers curl
around the sweet
palm-sized plastic.

Clicking mouse,
tapping keys,
soothe
my cyber-homesick soul.

Automatically, I click and log
onto social media.
It's been sooooooooo long.

The computer's clock says
four-fifty-one.
Four minutes to scroll,
five minutes to enter codes.
No problem.
As easy as trapping a level-one goblin.

Wow.
Reagan Whitfield,
dance team captain,
is no longer dating
our eighth-grade home-run hitter.
Fire Canyon Middle School
must be tilting sideways.

Four-fifty-four.
One minute more...

I scroll faster.
Holy moldy mutants!
Liam posted a photo
with Chris and Sawyer,
grudge-match enemies.
More photos of the three of them.
Fire Canyon's universe
has shifted into alien status.

Marcus Clawson posted
a video of his dog peeing
on his cat.
Hil-ar-i-ous.
I watch it again.
And again.
And again.

"Time to log off."
Rhino Librarian's
oniony-pickle breath wheezes.
She's standing behind me,
way too close.

"I'm almost done."
I exit,
speed-type
Show Low Chamber of Commerce.

Computer screen goes black.

Game Over

No, no, no, no, noooooo.
My heart skids
into my ribs.
Bolts of *what-have-I-done*
zap like those heart-shocker paddles.
I pound the keyboard.

Rhino Librarian clamps a bony hoof
on my shoulder. "Not a good idea."

"You've got to
turn the computer back on.
I need—"

"The computers
shut down on their own
at closing time.
I warned you."

Did she?

I walk out on
gummy bear legs.
How could I, the tech-meister,
botch entering simple scavenger hunt codes
on a freakin' website?
So stinkin' simple
a kindergartener could do it.
But apparently not me.

"Hey, Puke Pants.

Did you get in the codes?"
I recognize the voice.
Jordan.
Sheriff Show Low's kid.

Anger rolls.
Anger at Jordan
for messing with me.
Again.
Anger at Fey and Allen
for dumping the code-thing on me.
Molten lava anger because
I.
Screwed.
Up.
Again.

The blame train chugs into my station.
Again.

Press the Delete Key

Allen's gonna kill me.
Fey's gonna kill me.
I would kill me.

Outside, I slump onto a bench.
The sun's orange rays slide
through the pine trees and
the smell of smoke tingles my nose.
Must be the stink of
my karma cooking.

Allen plops on the bench.
"So did we win?"
His voice is chipmunk-chipper.

I squash any expression.
Don't want my face squealing.
"How would I know if we won?"

"Something wrong?"

"Why would anything be wrong?"

"Cause you're all Oscar the Grouch,
and you're sweating. A lot."

"What are you?
The perspiration police?
I've been running all day.
In the hottest state.
In July."

Then you guys ditched me.
Leaving five hundred bucks
on the line.
That's enough heat
to melt a lizard."

"Sorry.
You saw my mom," Allen says.
"She was worked up to crazy-times-ten."
He bounces on the bench.
And I feel sick.

"Where'd Fey go?" he asks.
You try to hold her hand again?"

"You jealous?"

"Forget it," Allen says
as if he's pressed the delete key.
"Girls. You can't trust 'em."

I don't want to talk about
trust.

Hippo-sized Lies

Driving to Ponderosa Pines,
Pops says, "You wanna tell me
why you're squeezed as tight
as a pair of vise grips?"

"I'm fine."
Which is a hippo-huge lie.

He parks beside Sheila.
"Told Earl I'd help
level his trailer.
Thought you might
want to work the jack."

"I'm kinda tired."

"Okay. Take Sheila.
I'll walk to Earl's."

Inside Trailer 13,
I flop on the sofa,
stare at the ceiling,
and figure out ways
to hitchhike
to Canada.

Mystery Box

On the counter.
Addressed to me.
From Mom.

I open the box.
Whoa.
A brand-new computer tablet.
I scan the features,
grab a knife
to slit
the plastic wrap,
but those vise grips of Pops
grab my stomach and
squeeze.

I don't deserve a new tablet.
I don't even deserve to look at the tablet.
I throw a dishtowel over the tablet.

I read Mom's note.

Dear Hertz,

Miss you.
Miss Avis.
Miss Phoenix.

Training with the new dog is going great.
She's feisty.
She'll keep your mom young.
I'm thinking we'll call her Budget. :)

I know your month of punishment
isn't up, but
Pops called and
said what a great kid you are.
Which I know.

Here's something
to ease your
homesickness
and likely your
boredom.
Just don't spend
every waking minute on it.
And don't fall asleep on it.

Love, Mom

Now my heart hurts,
my eyes leak,
and I know
what I have to do
to
make things right.

Can't fix what happened
in Phoenix.
But maybe
I can fix
losing the
scavenger hunt.

I need two-thirds
of the $500 prize
to give

to Allen and Fey.
I'll return the tablet.

Customer Service

I find
Phoebe,
Pops's flip phone.
She's still dead.
I unearth the charger from
under the sink
behind a bottle of bleach.
I plug Pheobe in and call
the number on the tablet box.

"Your call is important to us.
Please stay on the line.
This call may be monitored
for quality assurance."
Numb-your-ears muzak plays.
Forever.

I decide to write
Mom
a thank-you-postcard
while I wait.

Doe and Fawn Postcard

Coues Deer is a species of white-tailed deer that range along the **Arizona** Mogollon Rim.
Scientific name: ***Odocileus virginianus***.

Dear Mom,

Thanks for the tablet.
Miss you heaps and heaps.
More than you know.

Love,
Hertz and Avis

Kurt is Really Rajiv

"Good afternoon.
My name is Kurt.
How may I help you?"
Kurt's accent sounds
friendly and kind.
Like he's petting kittens.

Do the right thing.
Do the right thing.
"I need to return
a tablet my mom got me."

"Is there a problem
with the functionality of the device?"

"No. The thing is…
I don't want it."
This lie is so big
it could choke a herd of hippos.

"Is there another product
you'd be interested in?"

The Zona Products commercials,
flash.
The sizzle of tech-possibilities
snakes in my veins.
My fingers twitch ready to
swipe,
type.

I shove my twitchy fingers
in my pocket.
My knuckles bang against
the penny-of-dumb.

"Kurt, what I really need
is a device
that can rewind time.
Have you got that there
where you are?"

I imagine him in a warehouse
stacked with techno-toys.
"Where are you anyway?"

"I am in a customer service call center
in Mumbai.
And I am very sorry
I am not aware
of any time-rewind device,
although, our research department
is always working on new products."
He says this super-serious
and I'm psyched
they could be working on time travel.

"Why is it you want to return your tablet?" Kurt asks.

I need to explain.
To someone.
To Kurt.
How I'm not a mega-loser.
How I'm trying to do the right thing.

"Kurt. You don't sound like a Kurt.
Is that your real name?"

There's a pause in Mumbai.
"My name's Rajiv."

"Rajiv, here's the truth," I say.
"I screwed up.
I screwed things up for
my mom,
my dog,
probably for Pops,
and now
for my two new almost-friends.
And one's a girl.
What I need is a do-over."

"Do-over.
Good word," Rajiv says.
"But I am afraid I cannot help you
with a do-over.
However,
with your original receipt,
you can return your tablet
to any one of our local distributers."

I check the box.
"I don't have the receipt."

"Perhaps, if you ask your mother—"

"No." I slap the counter,
plates rattle.
I breathe in

to corral some calm.
"I can't ask my mom.
I need to fix this.
Myself."

There's silence in Mumbai
and I think Rajiv might've
taken another call.
Then across a million miles he says,
"I would not normally recommend this
because of the invalidation of the warranty."
Rajiv's voice is low and spy-like.
"You could sell the tablet.
Perhaps to a family member."

Yeah, that's not happening.
I'm not about to explain
Pops and low-tech Ponderosa Pines.

Then I remember
ABC Pawn Shop
on Deuce of Clubs Drive.
I can sell the tablet there.
Do the right thing.
"Thanks, Rajiv.
You're a screw-up-savior."

Let's Make a Deal

Avis drools,
adding his slime
to the grime
of the window of
ABC Pawn Shop.

I'm drooling, too,
peering through smeared glass,
at laptops, phones, and game systems.
And a sign—*Let's Make a Deal.*

Don't think about Blastoid Ball
or Cranium Crunchers
or Demolition Donkey.
Do the right thing.

"Okay, Avis. Sit. Stay."

Always obedient, Avis sits.
I go through a gate of iron bars.

There's one guy inside,
covered in tatts
with a beard thick enough
for rats to nest.

The store smells musty, funky,
the place is filled with
a jumble of
used camping gear,
a tangle of old electronics,

a skinny mannequin with no face
in a flight suit
pretending to play a drum set.

"Kid, didn't you read the sign?"
Tatt-man stands behind a glass case
of jewelry and guns.
The guns are scary.
But this guy's scarier.
His eyes say
he swallows live hamsters for lunch
and chases them down with hot sauce.

I dig down and
pull up my deepest Batman voice.
"I read the sign. I'm here to deal."

"Not that sign."
Tatt-man waves to a different dirty window.
"*No Unaccompanied Minors*.
Means unless you've got a grownup
in that bag you're shredding,
you gotta go."

I hold out the bag.
"Got a brand-new tablet."
My voice lost Batman and
gained Minnie Mouse.

Tatt-man strokes his rat-nest beard.
"That's something I might be interested in.
But I can't buy from anyone under eighteen.
It's county law.
Sheriff could put me outta—"

A mention of the sheriff,
and the door opens.
My legs quake,
the rest of my body jitters and shakes.
With my noodle luck
the sheriff has probably walked in
ready to arrest me
as a minor in the pawn shop.
Or there's still the arson stuff
he's trying to pin on me.

"Got anything new?"

I know that voice.
I glance back.
Not the sheriff.
The sheriff's son.
Jordan.

"Told you, Jordan,
you gotta be eighteen to be in here,"
Tatt-man says.

"Puke Pants isn't eighteen."
Jordan fires me a look of disgust,
like I'm flicking boogers.

"He's leaving."
Tatt-man takes a long look at my bag.

Jordan wanders further into the store.
"I'm almost eighteen."

Tatt-man rubs the back of his neck,

the skull tattoo on his bicep frowns.
"I'll give you both two minutes."
He points to my bag. "Let's see whatcha got."

I slide the bag across the glass.

Jordan slithers
around the edge of the store,
zeroes in on the camping equipment,
and an army-green camp stove.
"What kind of fuel burns in here?"

"Kerosene."
Tatt-man pulls out the unopened tablet.
He's trying for a poker face,
but his pupils stretch.
"I'd make you a deal on this,
but you gotta come back with an adult."

My shoulders sag.

Jordan picks up a silver lighter.
"Heard about another fire.
This one behind the library."
He shoots a cranium-crunching glare at me.
"Weren't you hanging around the library, Puke Pants?
Or should I call you Phoenix Firebug?"

Tatt-man jerks a thumb to the door.
"Time's up."

I wiggle past Jordan,
and I'm pretty sure
he slips the lighter

into his pocket.

Tatt-man's checking his phone.

I've made a mess of mistakes lately,
but I'm not dumb enough
to accuse the sheriff's son
of shoplifting.

The Note

Back at Ponderosa Pines
Avis scarfs his dinner
as if he hasn't eaten since Christmas.
Then stretches out under the trailer
in his worn-in dirt patch.

Pops is on another handy-helper job,
but he left me a plate of spaghetti,
two mega meatballs,
and a *Field and Stream* magazine,
with a sticky note.
See page 38. I know a spot.
We could take your friends.

He might mean Fey and Allen.
But until I fix
my screw up—
get them the money
due from the hunt—
we're likely not friends.

On page thirty-eight,
"Hooking Bass in Arizona."
A black-striped fish
sails over a rushing river
with a feathery hook
dangling from its mouth.

I devour the spaghetti,
and the striped-fish article.
The guy who wrote it

makes fishing sound as cool
as vanquishing video game Vikings.

I open the door.
"Avis? Want a meatball?"
Avis would eat the magazine if I
put spaghetti sauce on it.

No paws hitting dirt.
No panting.
No tail wagging.
No Avis.

I check his spot,
under his dish,
a note.

Got your dog.
Come to the lumberyard.
Alone.
Bring the tablet.
Let's make a deal.

Someone. Took. Avis.

Searing, scorching anger
ignites.
Cooking like
a potato too long in a microwave.
ready to explode.

Every muscle
from toes to teeth
clenches.
I crumple the note,
grab the ransom,
the tablet,
jump into Sheila.

Brain locks.
Got a fix on
who
took
Avis.

Only a few know
about the tablet—
Mom, Rajiv, Tatt-man.
And Jordan.

I mash the pedal,
peel over grass,
head to the park gate
and
slam on the brake.

Fey.
Blocking the gate.
She's a rattlesnake wound up,
ready to strike.
She smacks palms on Sheila.
"Where've you been?"

"Get out of the way,
I've got to go."

A venomous glare.
"Not until you tell me
what's with the hide-and-seek routine?"

"Not now. Move.
I've gotta save Avis."
My voice cracks on his name.

"What's happened to Avis?"
No more poison in her words.

"Someone took him.
I've got to go."

"Where?"

"The lumberyard."

"I'm going with you."
She's on the seat.

For a second,
I want her to come,
but I can't risk someone

messing with Avis.
He's been
traumatized enough
because of me.

"No. You can't.
Note said I've got to come alone."

Fey's got a worried look.
But she presses her hacky sack
into my hand.
"Take this.
It's lucky."

She leans in,
kisses me, quick.
On. The. Lips.

And I don't even
want to wipe my mouth.

Closed and Locked

Show Low Cash and Carry.
Sign lit,
store dark.

Without weapons
or superpowers,
my only strategy—
stealth.

In the shadows,
I slink,
squeeze
through the gap
between locked gates.
Set senses to ninja.

Voices.
More than one.

Tiptoe.

Voices louder.

Need surveillance.

A ninja would leap
onto a lumber stack.

Un-ninja-like,
I heave and pull,
slip and drop,

breathless and bruised,
haul myself up.
Lay flat.
Force short fortifying breaths.
Force myself to be brave.

I peek.
Rows of stacked lumber,
unfinished woodsheds,
a skid of unpainted doghouses,
a rusted forklift.
Beyond the back fence is
Pete's back door,
and below,
Jordan,
Matt,
Avis.

Kiss the Flame

"How long before the kid gets here?"
Matt yanks a rope
tied to Avis's collar.

Avis's head jerks.
His ears flatten.
His neck stretches.
His nose lifts and sniffs.
He knows I'm here.
He smells my fear.

"Puke Pants'll come," Jordan says.
He pulls out the pawn shop lighter.
Metal flint scrapes.
Jordan stares,
mesmerized by the miniature blaze.
Brings the lighter
to his lips as if
he's going to kiss the flame.
Then blows it out.

Air whooshes from my lungs.
Now I know.
Jordan, the sheriff's son,
is the dumpster arsonist.

Fire behind the Friendship Hall.
Fire at the Chamber of Commerce.
Fire at the library.
Stealing the lighter from the Pawn Shop.
Setting me up as his fall guy.

The Phoenix Firebug.

Psycho Sidekick

Matt unzips a backpack.
"You sure the kid won't call the cops?"

"I'm sure. Puke Pants twitches
whenever he hears mention of my dad."

"Good. And there're no security cameras," Matt says.

"Who'd steal lumber?" Jordan says.

"And if the kid doesn't show,
we can always just barbecue the mutt."
Matt's voice is ordinary,
like he's ordering his usual burger combo,
not threatening to kill my dog.

A skeleton fist squeezes my guts.
I need to be brave.
I need to get down,
give them the tablet,
and they'll give me Avis.
Maybe.

From the backpack, Matt pulls out
a small towel,
a plastic bottle.
He ties the towel to the end of Avis's rope,
pours liquid from the bottle
on the towel,
and flicks an orange plastic lighter.

"What are you doing?" Jordan asks.

"Toasting us a hot dog."

My stomach drops
through eight feet of stacked lumber,
it hits gravel,
and crashes to the center of the earth.

"No more yawny
dumpster fires
for me."
Matt holds the lighter
to the soaked towel.
"A flick of flame,
kerosene-soaked towel
ignites,
the dumb dog runs,
and all this wood turns
into a legendary inferno."

He twirls the lighter
playing with the
deadly device.

"Best thing.
I'm the sheriff's son's buddy," he says,
"I'll never be blamed.
They'll blame
The Phoenix Firebug."

I was wrong.
Jordan isn't the only arsonist.
Matt, his sidekick, is pyro-psycho.

Rusty Forklift

The seams holding in my fear rip,
rage detonates.
I scramble backwards,
drop off the wood stack.

What I need is hover shoes or
a Black Hawk helicopter
or an X-wing fighter.
I throw the hacky sack one way
as a distraction
and take off for the only thing I do have—
the rusty forklift.

"It's Puke-Pants!
Let's get the tablet
and get outta here."
Jordan's tone isn't an order, it's a plea.

"No chance." Matt's voice.

Feet crunch on gravel.

I hurl rocks
every direction as I run,
hoping to confuse and
divert.

I jump on the forklift
and pray
harder than on the days
my report cards come home

that there's a key.

Yes.
Please start. Please start. Please start.

The engine rumbles,
louder than any golf cart.

Not a Helicopter

I'm praying again,
that driving a forklift
is the same as driving Sheila.

I rev the gas.
Black smoke belches.
The engine grumbles.

The forklift's jammed
against a stack of lumber.
I search for reverse,
find R on the shift stick
remember about clutches,
shift,
ease the gas,
coast backwards.

I clutch, shift,
find first gear.
The forklift rolls,
snail-crawl slow.

So not a Black Hawk helicopter.
But me on a rusted hunk of metal
is a trillion times better
than me alone
taking on psycho, pyro-nut Matt.
Where is he?
Where's Avis?

Tonka Toy

Matt slides around
a skid of dog houses
with Avis,
the rope,
soaked towel,
lighter.

I've got to
save Avis.
Save the lumberyard.
Save Show Low
from Matt's nightmare fire.

"Look what I found."
He holds up the tablet—
the ransom
I dropped.
He doesn't look worried
or nervous.
He looks like
he's king
and me
on an old forklift
is as terrifying as a mouse
with a toothpick-sword.

"Let. Avis. Go."
My panic gets flattened
between my clenched teeth.

Two more levers

on the forklift dash.
I grab one and pray.
The man-sized steel forks rise.
I stop at
decapitation height.

A peewee droplet of worry creeps
over Matt's face.
"You done playing
with your Tonka toy?
'Cuz I'm ready
for a bar-be-cue."

Fury swells.
I stomp the gas,
but the forklift
still rolls centipede-slow.

Matt baby steps backward.

I shift the forks up,
down.

He laughs.
"Oh no.
The big bad forklift
might mess my hair."

I'm desperate for more.
For cannons.
For rocket boosters.
For a laser launch switch.

I spy a button labeled *Road* and

press.
The forklift blasts off,
fishtails,
and the back-end smashes lumber.
Wood cracks.
Boards bounce.

"Whaaaaaaaaat?" Matt squeals
like he got crotch-kicked,
dives behind wood sheds,
dragging Avis.

My slick hands slip.
Beeeeeep.
A horn.
Someone's got to hear
my get-help honks.

Trapped

I zoom the yard
beeping,
honking,
searching for Matt.
Gotta find Avis.

Finally.
At the back fence,
between Pete's Place,
Matt and Jordan,
ready to climb.

No Avis.
He must've got away.

I aim the forks
at Matt's head.
A warning.

Caught between me and the fence,
no more peewee worry,
no more mouse with a toothpick.
Matt's dump-a-load-in-his-shorts scared.

Jordan leaps onto a skid of lumber.
Matt does too and
he salutes. "Later."
He lifts his nose.
"What's that I smell?
Burning dog?"

A jagged blade of anger slices,
and I bleed fury.

Going Up

I slam forward the lever
to the hydraulic-pistons-of-death.
The forks drop,
cracking gravel,
bouncing so hard
my teeth rattle.

I drive the prongs under
the skid
holding Jordan and Matt.
The skid rocks.
Jordan falls, butt-smacks.
Matt staggers.

I lift and shift into reverse,
back up,
hoist higher and higher and higher.

Twelve feet up,
eight feet back from the fence,
fifty miles from their fearlessness.

I push the last lever,
the stack tips.
Jordan screams.
Matt scrambles
to hang on,
drops the tablet,
smack and crack.

"What's going on?"

Pete at the diner's back door.

"The kid's crazy," Jordan says.
"But Matt's psycho. Call my dad."

Suspended

"Jordan's right,"
I yell to Pete.
"Call the sheriff."

Should I lower Matt and Jordan?
Or leave them suspended?
I eye the forklift lever—
leave it where it is.

I leap off the seat.

Must find Avis.

Pops to the Rescue

Gravel pings,
dust flies,
"Star Spangled Banner" blasts.

Anastasia careens
into the parking lot.
Pops somehow knew.
Fey knew.

I shout and wave and holler.

The huge Cadillac barrels
at the locked gate,
metal rips and clangs.
Another Star-Spangled blast.
Headlights flash.

Anastasia swerves
around lumber
going NASCAR fast.
Too fast.
Hits the skid of doghouses,
which topple and smash.

I bolt
to a steaming Anastasia
buried in doghouses.

Pops and Fey—
frantic behind
a cracked windshield.

All four doors jammed
against doghouses.

"Where's Avis?" Fey yells.

Pops tries every door.

"I don't know," I say.
"Matt's trying to set
the lumberyard on fire.
With Avis."

"Go," Pops says.
"Find Avis."

Praying to the Dog Gods

He's gonna be fine.
He's gonna be okay.
Another plea to the dog gods.
Like before.

A rat in a maze,
I search and scream.
"Aaaaaaa-vis."
Where would he go?

Avis is smart.
Super-smart.
Where would a super-smart dog,
with a burning towel
tied to his collar go?

I bite back tears.
He's here.
Somewhere.

He'd try to get out.
I race to the gate.
No Avis.

WOOF

A bark karate chops my heart.

I run
to the woofs.
Around lumber.
Along the fence.
And there's
Avis.
And the rope
tied to his collar
with
the kerosene-soaked towel
on FIRE.

Avis jumps and barks,
claws at the fence.
Nails click-clacking against
chain-link.

I'm shaking and sweating and shivering,
pocketknife in hand.
Fingers wobbly, fumbly,
like cooked noodles,
I pull the biggest blade.
"It's okay. It's okay.
I'm gonna cut the rope."

But now the rope's burning.
I'll get burned.
Doesn't matter—
burns heal.

I step closer.

Avis spins,
flaming rope whips,
singeing fur.

"It's okay!"
But it isn't.

Avis paws at the fence,
frantic.

And I see.

Avis isn't super-smart,
he's a canine Einstein.

FAUCET VALVE

      twist

      turn

      turn

squeeze the sprayer and pray that

in the water versus kerosene battle

winner is   W

Shower of   A

flames   T

fizzle   E

water   R

 works   !

Avis is   !

SAVED.   !

         I collapse in a puddle of relief.

Apology Accepted

Blue lights flash,
Sherriff arrives.

Jordan stuck like
a cat up a tree
meows a confession.

Matt stays as mute
as a bark beetle.

Pete produces
video
from his
parking lot
security camera
hands to the sheriff.

Jordan and Matt
are lowered
and stowed in
the patrol car.

Then Sherriff Show Low
fixes his laser glare
on me.
But instead of the usual
I-know-you're-to-blame
expression,
he's wearing an
I-might've-messed-up
face.

And I feel
a little sorry for him.
Because I've got
lots of experience
wearing that face.

Then he says,
"Hertz, I'm
soooorrrrr-gr-gr-grrr."
The snarled word
might be
sorry?

Pops pounces.
"What was that, Sheriff?
My hearing isn't what
it used to be."

Sheriff Show Low's
jaw loosens.
"Just letting Hertz
know I owe him
an apology."

Pops quirks a rodent eyebrow.
"Might be you owe him
more than just one.
I recall several accusations
flying around town."

I expect Sheriff Show Low
to arrest Pops on the spot.

Instead, the sheriff says,

"Okay, maybe
I owe two
or three apologies.
Sorry."
His sorry sticks
like peanut butter
to the roof of his mouth.
"I'll let
Crime Stoppers know
you saved the lumberyard, Hertz."

Fey nudges and whispers
"I bet there's a reward."

Puffed Up with Pride

I'm thinking,
be cool
act cool
cool cool cool.
But my mind still
sees fur flames,
smells smoke,
envisions Avis on fire.

My fight juice drains.
Muscles go loose
and stretchy like Plastic Man.
I'm afraid
I may
dissolve
into a
puddle of gooey
ohnoohnoohno
feelings.

Then,
Avis licks
my skin.
His eyes say
I knew you'd
save the day.

I hug him hard.
He feels so solid,
and now I do too.

Pete invites us in,
cooks up
pancake sundaes for
Fey, Allen, Carlos, Pops, me
and
a special plate
for Avis.
No cherries.

Roadrunner Postcard

The **Roadrunner** is **Arizona's** iconic bird and largest cuckoo which can reach speeds of 20mph.
Scientific name: ***Geococcyx californianus***

Dear Mom,

Avis and I
made the news again.
And it's good news.
This time,
we didn't start a fire—
we stopped one.
And we got a reward!

Love Hertz and Avis

PS: did you get insurance on
*   the tablet?*

Crime Stopper Cash

With wads of crisp twenties,
me, Allen, and Fey
invade ABC Pawn Shop.

Tatt-man shoots me his best
Sasquatch get-out-of-my-forest glare.

I hold up my palms.
"I've got the over-eighteen guy.
He's so old he could count as five grownups."

Pops strolls in,
navy shorts,
Proud Veteran t-shirt,
Home of the Brave ball cap.
"Sorry kids, saw an RCA TV in the window.
Radio Corporation of America—
talk about a fantastic American-owned company."
Pops practically salutes. "Well...
until Sony bought them."

Allen bounds between
the drum set and video games.
"Great place to spend our winnings."

"Technically, not winnings."
Fey takes the earflap hat off
flyer-guy mannequin.
"We should've, could've won.
We had all the clues and codes."
She puts on the hat

and grins at me.
Her smile's wider
than Tatt-Man's shoulders,
telling me she's not mad.

Allen whacks a cymbal on the
drum set. "Hertz made up for it,
splitting his Crime Stoppers cash."

"Maybe the three of us
could start a band."
Fey strums a guitar.

Maybe the band thing?
I could buy an instrument,
except
my fifth-grade music teacher, Mrs. Mancini
declared me tone deaf.
So, trying to look cool
for Fey
in a band
would likely land me
a solid ten out of ten
on the humiliation scale.

No Tech Wonders

Pops drapes his arm on my shoulders,
"You getting some screeny gizmo?"

Used laptops, tablets, cellphones beckon.
But I learned weird and wondrous
un-techy stuff
in Show Low, Arizona.

Like how to change a thermostat,
and how to drive a golf cart
and how to use a forklift.
It turns out staying
with an unusual relative
may not be torture,
and I can make friends
in strange places,
like an Airstream trailer park
or lumberyard.
A cute girl
kissed me.
Not even as a dare.
And I even caught a couple arsonists.
Show Low is
definitely not Dullsville.

Pops picks up a fishing rod.
flicks his wrist,
"Nice action."
I remember the *Field and Stream* article,
take hold of a pole.
The cork handle is

light and cool,
not hard and hot
like a game controller.
"You think I could
catch a fish with this rod?"

Pops checks the logo.
"A *Falcon*. All American.
I'd say you'd have a good shot at a big bass
or trout.
And you'll need this."
He opens a tan toolbox,
lets out a whistle.
Trays with hooks and feathers,
fake fish, fake worms, fake frogs.
Pops dangles an orange and black feathered hook.
"Bass can't resist this buck-tailed spinner."

"Looks like an earring."
Fey takes off the flight hat,
puts on a cap with the words
"To Fish or Not to Fish?
What a Stupid Question."

Allen, arms loaded with
old-school video games, says,
"You don't need that stuff.
We can play *Cabela's Big Bad Bass*."

The sight of video games
pokes my sleeping techie bear.
I steal a glance at the window
loaded with used tech toys.

"You say Cabela's?" Pops asks.
"Best ever all-American hunting and fishing store."
He hands Allen a fishing rod.
"But try the real thing."

Allen swings the rod
like a baseball bat.

"With those poles, you boys
look like natural-born fishermen."
Pops sounds puffed-out-chest proud.

Hooked

"Fishing?
We should definitely do it."
Fey says, still wearing the
fish-or-not-to-fish hat,
and a vest with fifty-five pockets.
Her eyes glow green-light bright.

And I'm in trouble.
Godzilla-sized trouble.
Not the cleaning-toilets-til-I'm-a-hundred trouble.
Not the no-allowance-in-this-millennium trouble.
Worse.
Girl trouble.

Forget laptops or tablets or video games,
my cash is going to fishing gear.

At the register,
Tatt-man totals me up.
"Comes to eighty dollars and one cent."

I count out four twenties
and then reach deep
in my pocket.
My fingers hit
the Dork of Dumb penny
Sweaty Fireman threw at me.
I pull it out
and present it to Tatt-man.
"Time to ditch this souvenir."

ACKNOWLEDGMENTS

Hertz Gets Fused coming to you has been a long journey. The story began with 50,000 words in prose written during National November Writing Month (NaNoWriMo). Then in July, a group of fabulous writers were the first to read some of *Hertz* at a writers' immersion in Atlanta, Georgia. These brave women actually acted out the first pages, and we laughed until we cried and our sides ached. Thank you to Alison Stone, Kennedy Ryan, Darcy Crowder, Brenna Lauren, and Jaki Towns. Huge hugs to Margie Lawson for organizing the immersion, your support and critiques of *Hertz*, for presenting oodles of rhetorical devices which led me to free verse poetry, and the inspiration for naming Hertz's dog—Avis.

Hertz never would've happened if it hadn't been for my wonderful, adventurous in-laws, Bob and Mary June Purvis for introducing me to Show Low, Arizona, and their Airstream park.

With deep appreciation and heart-felt thanks to my fantastic writer friends who offered tireless support: Sandra Tilley, Brenda Spears Mania, Robin Wiesneth, Lisa Black, and Lauri Corkum.

To some of my amazing writing teachers and workshop leaders over the years, Margie Lawson, Joyce Sweeney, Devon Ellington, Linda Sue Park, Marc Olmsted, Kelly Bingham, and Cordelia Jensen—I'm so grateful for the writerly growth you provided by sharing your wisdom.

I'm honored to work with the wonderful staff at Owl's Nest Publishers who adore *Hertz* as much as I do. To my editors Katie Stewart, Ash Schlax, and Karin Hoyle thank you for your smart, thoughtful edits which allowed *Hertz* to shine even brighter. And many thanks to Ash for a stunning cover design.

Lastly, my family—there are no words with enough heart to thank James Purvis, my compassionate, heroic husband, Jessica and Skylar, my dazzling and accomplished kids: you never doubted me or Hertz's story, even when I did. I love you to the stars and beyond.

ABOUT THE AUTHOR

Suzanne Purvis is a transplanted Canadian living in the Deep South, where she traded "eh" for "y'all." She's an author of long, short, flash fiction, and poetry for both children and adults, often written with a touch of humor. When not writing, she can usually be found on, in, or near the water; kayaking with dolphins, snorkeling with rays, swimming in the Gulf, and even parasailing above the waves. She finds inspiration at home in the often forgotten northwest corner of Florida with her husband and two dogs, Winkin and Ozzie.

You can find Suzanne at www.suzannepurvis.com

Thank you for reading this Owl's Nest book! We hope you enjoyed it. Please consider leaving a review on Amazon, Goodreads, or sharing about the book on social media!

You can find and follow Owl's Nest Publishers on social media by searching for @owlsnestpublishers.

Find extras, merch, our mailing list, our podcast, and other great middle grade, teen, poetry, and classic books at owlsnestpublishers.com!

This is the Owl's Nest; come in and read.

Made in United States
Orlando, FL
19 May 2023